THE CASE
OF THE
PECULIAR PINK FAN

THE CASE
OF THE
PECULIAR PINK FAN

AN ENOLA HOLMES MYSTERY

NANCY SPRINGER

PHILOMEL BOOKS

To my mother

PHILOMEL BOOKS
A division of Penguin Young Readers Group. Published by The Penguin Group.
Penguin Group (USA) Inc., 375 Hudson Street, New York, NY 10014, U.S.A.
Penguin Group (Canada), 90 Eglinton Avenue East, Suite 700, Toronto, Ontario M4P 2Y3,
Canada (a division of Pearson Penguin Canada Inc.).
Penguin Books Ltd, 80 Strand, London WC2R 0RL, England.
Penguin Ireland, 25 St. Stephen's Green, Dublin 2, Ireland (a division of Penguin Books Ltd).
Penguin Group (Australia), 250 Camberwell Road, Camberwell, Victoria 3124, Australia
(a division of Pearson Australia Group Pty Ltd).
Penguin Books India Pvt Ltd, 11 Community Centre, Panchsheel Park,
New Delhi - 110 017, India.
Penguin Group (NZ), 67 Apollo Drive, Rosedale, North Shore 0632, New Zealand
(a division of Pearson New Zealand Ltd).
Penguin Books (South Africa) (Pty) Ltd, 24 Sturdee Avenue, Rosebank,
Johannesburg 2196, South Africa.
Penguin Books Ltd, Registered Offices: 80 Strand, London WC2R 0RL, England.

Published simultaneously in Canada. Printed in the United States of America.
Design by Marikka Tamura.
Library of Congress Cataloging-in-Publication Data
Springer, Nancy. The case of the peculiar pink fan : an Enola Holmes mystery / Nancy Springer.
p. cm. Summary: Fourteen-year-old Enola Holmes, younger sister of the famous detective,
Sherlock, endeavors to save her friend Lady Cecily from an arranged marriage.
[1. Arranged marriage—Fiction. 2. Lost and found possessions—Fiction.
3. Characters in literature—Fiction. 4. London (England)—History—19th century—Fiction.
5. Great Britain—History—19th century—Fiction.
6. Mystery and detective stories.] I. Title.
PZ7.S76846Cat 2008 [Fic]—dc22 2008006933
ISBN 978-0-399-24780-4
1 3 5 7 9 10 8 6 4 2

May, 1889

"It has now been more than eight months since the girl went missing—"

"The girl has a name, my dear Mycroft," interrupts Sherlock with only a slight edge in his voice, mindful that he is his brother's dinner-guest. Mycroft, an excellent host despite his reclusive ways, has waited until the wood-pigeon pie with currant sauce has been despatched before addressing the unpleasant problem of their youthful sister, Enola Holmes.

"Enola. Nor, alas, did she go missing in any usual sense of the term," adds Sherlock in quieter, almost whimsical tones. "She rebelled, she bolted, and she has actively eluded us."

"But that is not all she has actively done." Grunting as his frontal amplitude gets in his way, My-croft leans forward and reaches for the cut-glass decanter.

Aware that Mycroft has something of essence to say, Sherlock waits silently while his older brother refills their glasses with the excellent beverage that is making this conversation palatable. Both men have loosened their high starched collars and black ties.

Mycroft sips his drink before he continues speaking in his usual ponderous and irritating way. "During that eight-month period of time she has been instrumental in rescuing three missing persons, and in bringing three dangerous criminals to justice."

"I had noticed," Sherlock acknowledges. "What of it?"

"Do you not detect a most alarming pattern in her activities?"

"Not at all. Sheerest happenstance. The case of the Marquess of Basilwether she stumbled across. Lady Cecily Alistair she found while administering charity upon the streets in her guise as a nun. And—"

"And she just *happened* to be able to identify the kidnapper?"

Sherlock stares down Mycroft's acid comment. "And, as I was going to say, concerning Watson's disappearance, if he were not so publicly linked with me, would she have become involved?"

"You do not know how or why she became involved. You still do not know how she found him."

"No," admits Sherlock Holmes, "I do not." Partially due to the mellowing influence of his brother's well-aged port wine, and partially due to the passing of time and certain events that have occurred, thoughts of his runaway sister no longer cause him sharp chagrin and even more keen anxiety. "And it is not the first time she has outwitted me," he says, almost with pride.

"Bah. What good will such tricks and temerity do her when she becomes a woman?"

"Little enough, I suppose. She is a true daughter of our Suffragist mother. But at least for the moment, I no longer fear for her safety. Evidently she is quite able to take care of herself."

Mycroft gestures as if brushing away an irritating insect. "That is not the point. It is the girl's future that is at stake, not her immediate survival. What is to become of her in a few years? No gentleman of any means will wed such an independent young woman who interests herself in criminal activities!"

"She is only fourteen, Mycroft," Sherlock points out patiently. "When she reaches courting age, I doubt she will any longer carry a dagger in her bosom."

Mycroft arches his thorny eyebrows. "You think she will eventually conform to society's expectations? You, who refused to take a degree in any recognised field, instead inventing your own calling and livelihood?"

The world's first and only private consulting detective gestures dismissively. "She is *female,* my dear Mycroft. The biological imperatives of her sex urge her to nest and procreate. The first stirrings of womanly maturity will impel her—"

"Bah! Balderdash!" Mycroft can no longer restrain his asperity. "You really think our renegade sister will settle down to find herself a husband—"

"Why, what do you think she will do?" retorts Sherlock, a bit stung; the great detective is unaccustomed to the word *balderdash* as applied to his pronouncements. "Perhaps she intends to make a life-long career of finding missing persons and apprehending evildoers?"

"It is possible."

"What, you believe she might set herself up in business? As my competition?" Sherlock's annoyance gives way to amusement; he begins to chuckle.

Mycroft says quietly, "I would not put it beyond her."

"You'll have her smoking cigars next!" Sherlock Holmes laughs heartily now. "Have you forgotten our sister is just a wayward child? She cannot possibly possess such fixity of purpose. Preposterous, my dear Mycroft, utterly preposterous!"

CHAPTER
THE
FIRST

SO FAR, MY ONLY CLIENTS AS "DR. RAGOSTIN, Scientific Perditorian" had been a stout, elderly widow anxious to find her lost lapdog; a frightened lady who could not locate a valuable heart-shaped ruby which had been given to her by her husband; and an army general whose most cherished souvenir of the Crimean War had disappeared, namely, his bullet-riddled leg-bone signed by the field doctor who had amputated it.

Trifles, all. My energies should have been directed towards a far more important objective: to find Mum. I knew my mother was roaming with the Gypsies, and I had promised myself that in the spring I would track her down, not to reproach her or coerce her, only to reunite with my—my amputated family member, so to speak.

Yet here it was May already, I had made no effort at all to search for Mum, and I did not know why except to say that business detained me in London.

Business? A lapdog, a lapidary, and a leg-bone?

But clients were clients, I told myself. It had not, of course, been necessary (or possible) for any of them to meet the illustrious (and fictitious) Dr. Ragostin himself. Rather, "Miss Ivy Meshle," his trusted assistant, had returned the widow's pet, an adorable curly-haired spaniel, to its grateful owner, having taken it back from a notorious Whitechapel dealer in purloined purebred dogs. Similarly, "Miss Meshle" had resolved the affair of the lost jewel simply enough by sending a boy up the linden tree outside the lady's window to look in a magpie's nest. (How easily I could have climbed that tree myself, and how I yearned to do so! But propriety forbade.) As for the general's leg-in-a-box, I was rather tepidly on the trail of it when I chanced to become involved in a far more intriguing and, as it turned out, urgent case.

I blush to confess that the initial encounter took place within a recent establishment on Oxford Street which, while gratefully patronised by gentlewomen who shopped that expensive district, was not mentioned in mixed society: the first London Ladies' Lavatory.

This splendid innovation, tacitly acknowledging

that well-bred women no longer spent their days at home within a few steps of their own water-closets, cost a penny to enter—quite worth it, when one needed it, even though the same sum would have given an East End child bread, milk, and grammar-schooling for a day. The cost ensured that the facility was used mostly by females of the upper classes, although the occasional working-girl, such as Ivy Meshle in her false curls and cheaply fashionable ready-made clothing, might venture in.

That day, however, I was not disguised as the slightly vulgar Ivy Meshle. Instead, my inquiries having taken me into the neighbourhood of the British Museum—which both of my brothers frequented, to my discomfiture—I was got up as a female scholar, with my unlovely hair in a plain bun and my narrow, sallow face disguised by ebony-rimmed spectacles. These, while minimising my alarming nose, also made me an object rather beneath notice, as no fashionable lady would ever wear glasses. In a dress of good-quality yet narrow, dark, and untrimmed serge, and a similarly plain dark hat, I sat in the Ladies' Lavatory's comfortably dark brown-leather-and-faux-marble parlour to relax a few moments in grateful certainty that neither Sherlock nor Mycroft was likely to come in there after me.

It had been a fraught day so far—female scholars are not much admired among the male populace of

London—but here I attracted no attention; it was quite customary for a patron weary of shopping to rest in the parlour's shadowy plasterwork coolness before venturing again into the dust and heat of the street.

A bell tinkled, the maidservant crossed the lavatory parlour to open the door, and three ladies came in. They passed close by me, for I occupied a plush russet settee beside the door. I did not, of course, look up from my newspaper, nor would I have given them any thought if it were not that, from the moment they entered, I sensed something amiss, badly so. A tension amongst them.

I heard silk petticoats rustling as they passed, but no other sound. They were not speaking to one another.

Wondering what might be the matter, without moving my head (it would have been bad manners to peer openly) I raised my eyes, although I could tell little enough from my view of their backs.

Two richly dressed matrons, their voluminous skirts trailing, flanked a younger, slimmer female in the very latest Paris fashion—indeed, it was the first time I had seen a bell skirt on an actual person rather than a department-store mannequin. Huge citrine bows poufed and trailed by way of a bustle or train, but the skirt itself, of a deeper yellow-green, was drawn in by hidden tapes as if to simulate a second waist in the neighbourhood of the knees. Beneath this, it spread out again to form a flounced "bell" from under which the girl's feet never peeped; indeed, they hardly stirred her ruffles as she walked, for her skirt limited her stride to perhaps ten inches. I winced, watching her falter along, for—although her slender form did not attain the ideal "hourglass" figure—to my eye she was a lovely creature; it was as if someone had put a deer in hobbles. Good sense had always sacrificed itself for fashion, of course—hoop skirts, bustles—but this girl, I thought, must utterly be fashion's fool, wearing a dress in which she could barely toddle!

As the trio neared the doorway to the lavatory's inner sanctum, the girl halted.

"Come along, child," commanded one of the older women.

Instead, without a word, the bell-skirted girl seated herself less than gracefully. Indeed, she threw herself, almost falling, into one of the dark leather armchairs across the room from me.

And as her face turned towards me, I very nearly gasped aloud with shock and surprise, for I knew her! I could not be mistaken, for our adventures, the sisterhood I had felt for her, my terror when the garroter had attacked her, all remained indelibly in my memory; the sight of her sensitive, cultured face magnetised me. It was the baronet's daughter, the

left-handed lady whom I had once found and rescued—it was the Honourable Cecily Alistair.

But I did not recognise the women with
her. Where was Cecily's mother, the lovely Lady
Theodora?

As for Lady Cecily: this past winter I had seen
her cold, hungry, and dressed in rags, with all the
lustre gone out of her brilliant eyes, but nothing
could have prepared me for the alarm I felt at her
appearance now. Her face seemed even more haggard than when I had seen her last, and its expression
more distressed. With her jaw clenched and her full
lips thinned in defiance, with a glare of wild, desperate rebellion she faced the two matrons towering
over her.

"No, indeed, young lady," said one of these in au-
thoritative tones that declared her to be far more
than chaperone—grandmama, perhaps, or auntie?
"You are coming with us." She grasped the seated
girl by one elbow, and the second woman seized the
other.

By now I had raised my head, frankly gawking.
Luckily, the two dowagers faced away from me,
their attention all on the sixteen-year-old girl in the
armchair.

In a low voice Lady Cecily replied, "You cannot
make me," and she slumped deep in the chair, quite
smashing her citrine ornamentations, letting herself

sag with her head down so that, if the two women wanted her to stand, they must haul her bodily to her feet. This would have been no small struggle, yet I think they would have done so if it were not for my presence; they glanced around to see who might be watching. Hastily I looked down again at my newspaper, but they were not stupid.

"Well," I heard one of them say in brittle tones, "I suppose we must go by turns."

"Proceed," responded the other. "I will stay with her."

One of them then went into the lavatory proper, and hearing its door swing shut, I glanced up again. The second matron was seating herself upon another armchair, her attention for the moment fixed on the arrangement of her pongee draperies, and in that instant Lady Cecily lifted her head and, like a prisoner mindful of any possible means of escape, looked straight at me.

And recognised me. Even though we had met only once before, the night her kidnapper had nearly killed her, she knew me. *Snap*, it was as if a whip had cracked, such was the force with which our gazes met, and the speed, for instantly she looked down again, doubtless to hide from her companion the widening of her eyes.

Doing likewise, I wondered whether she remembered my name, which I had so impulsively and unwisely divulged to her: Enola Holmes. I felt sisterhood towards this unhappy genius, a baronet's daughter of dual personality: the left-handed artist who felt the plight of the poor and rendered it in the most extraordinary charcoal drawings, yet who was forced to be the docile right-handed Lady Cecily for society.

But I knew much more of her than she did of me; I could only imagine how much like a dream I, a mystery girl in a black cloak, must have seemed on that perilous night, and her incredulity at seeing me again, now, in daylight. And perhaps her hope that I might once again assist her, whatever her plight might be.

What might be the matter? Laying my newspaper aside as if I were tired of it, I considered the desperation I had seen in Lady Cecily's dark eyes, the pallor of her gaunt face, the dullness of her golden-brown hair pulled straight back from her forehead beneath a simple hat, a flat straw boater.

When, a moment later, I ventured to look up again, she held a fan.

A most peculiar fan, for it was uniformly candy pink—dreadfully common—and quite mismatched to her lemon ribbons, lime skirt, and creamy kid-leather gloves and boots. Also, while her expensive new skirt was of the finest butter-soft yellow-green surah, her fan was made of merest folded paper glued to plain sticks and edged with ordinary pink-tinted feathers.

Her dowager escort, seated close to her and at an angle to watch her, said peevishly, "I am sure I will never understand why you insist on dragging that awful thing around when you have that nice fan I gave you. Cream silk panne with carved ivory sticks and point-lace overlay; have you forgotten?"

Ignoring her, Cecily opened the pink fan and began to ply it as if to cool her face. I noticed that she used her left hand—significant; she chose to be her true self rather than obeying the demands of propriety. I noticed also that she positioned the fan as a frail sort of barrier between herself and her guardian. Behind its brief concealment her gaze caught mine, and in that moment the fan almost as if by accident tapped her on the forehead.

I understood her signal at once: *Caution. We are being watched.* The language of fans had been invented by young lovers attempting to court in the presence of chaperones, and while certainly I had never enjoyed a lover—nor did I expect I ever would—in my innocent childhood days at Ferndell Hall, and under the wry tutelage of my mother, I had often been diverted by watching.

Giving no other sign, I sighed as if hot and weary, reached into a large pocket centred under the frontal drapery of my dress, and pulled out my own fan, which I carried not for the sake of elegance or flirtation, but simply to cool my face. My fan was brown cambric, plain but tasteful, and I opened it far enough—more than halfway—to indicate friendship.

Meanwhile, the dowager who had gone into the lavatory emerged, and the other one rose to take her turn. Lady Cecily seized this moment, when their attention was distracted, to send her fan into a frenzied fluttering, clearly a signal of agitation and distress.

I let my fan rest for a moment upon my right cheek. *Yes.* Telling her that I understood; something was wrong.

"Use your right hand," snapped the dowager who was now seating herself, "and put that silly toy away."

Although she froze motionless, Cecily did not obey.

"Put it away, I said," ordered her—captor? Such seemed to be the role of the dowager.

Lady Cecily said, "No. It amuses me."

"No?" The larger, older woman's tone became dangerous—but then shifted. "Oh, very well, defy me—but only in this." Lowering rather than raising her voice, she spoke on grimly yet so quietly that I could not hear. Stiffly seated—her stout waist corseted to the utmost within her elaborate gown—

the dowager kept her profile to me; and whilst outwardly I sat sedately fanning myself, inwardly my every sense had alerted like a hunting dog on point. Studying the woman before me so as to recognise her should I see her again, I realised it would be difficult to tell her from the other one; both had features oddly dainty amidst the breadth and fleshiness of their faces: arched, brittle brows, puppy noses, thin lips. Indeed, both looked so much alike that quite probably they were sisters, perhaps even twins. This one's hair might be greying a bit more than the other's, what I could see of it beneath a magnificent hat so tilted and convoluted that dog-tooth lilies clustered *beneath* its brim.

". . . if it takes all day." Her voice rose slightly as vehemence took hold. "A trousseau you will need, and a trousseau you shall have."

Lady Cecily said, "You cannot make me wear it."

"We shall see. Come along," she said as the other matron emerged from the lavatory, signalling her readiness by lifting her parasol.

Without a word Cecily stood up, but as she did so, she held her fan open in front of her face. Meant to encourage a timid lover, the fan so displayed signalled *Approach me.* But under the circumstances, with her great dark eyes flashing a plea to me over its pink-feathered edge, the fan signalled—what?

Do not forsake me.

Help me.

Willingly, I thought, as I tapped my cheek *Yes* — but how?

Rescue me.

From what?

"Do put that wretched toy in your pocket!"

Cecily only lowered her pink fan to her side as the two dowagers flanked her again and accompanied her towards the door beside which I sat with my fan languidly waving but my mind racing. Cecily held her fan by its string now, twirling it — another signal of danger. *Be careful. We are being watched.*

She wished for secrecy, then. So I acted abstracted, gazing at an ugly gilt-framed still-life on the far wall as they passed me, but all the time planning to follow them, find out where they —

Thump, an impact rocked the settee in which I sat, and peripherally I saw a blur of citrine — Lady Cecily — who had tripped over her ridiculous bell skirt, nearly falling into me. Instantly her two scowling escorts scooped her up and hurried her out, all without a word of apology to me.

Had they spared me even a glance, they might have seen as I did: on the settee next to me lay the pink paper fan.

CHAPTER
THE
SECOND

THE INSTANT THE DOOR CLOSED BEHIND CECILY and her two redoubtable chaperones, I sprang to my feet, slipping her pink fan along with my own into my pocket. I had to follow her and find out what was the matter in order to help her—but if I trailed her party too closely, I risked being noticed by her formidable chaperones. Therefore, I first jumped upon the settee, where by standing on tiptoe I could just see through the lavatory's high window. The deep-set diamond-shaped window-panes distorted my limited view, but I could make out the threesome progressing towards the cab-stand.

Climbing down, I found the maidservant watching me with her mouth open. Laying a finger to my lips, I handed her a shilling, buying her silence. This transaction delayed me only slightly, yet seemed to take forever; in great haste I pulled on my gloves and exited the lavatory. To my relief, I was just in time to see a slight figure in a bell skirt being helped into a four-wheeler along with her two guardians. Taking note mentally of their cab's number, I strode forward to secure one of my own —

But never got so far.

In that careless, unfortunate moment I found myself face-to-face with my brother.

The older, stouter one. Mycroft.

We all but bumped into each other, and were, I think, both equally startled. I believe I screamed. I know he let forth with a sort of hoot, as if someone had given him a hard blow to his stamped-velvet waistcoat. As everything happened at once, it is hard to recall who moved first, whether he seized me by the elbow before or after I kicked him briskly in the shin — but I know I twisted like an eel in his grip, I seem to recall stamping hard on the well-polished toe of his thin leather boot, and, without resorting to my dagger, I broke away and ran.

Had he been Sherlock, very likely freedom would have been all over for me, but it was not hard to run from Mycroft. I heard him puff after me only a few steps before he bellowed to all and sundry, "Stop that girl!"

Simultaneously I shrieked, "That man laid hands upon me!" An accusation so shocking that bystanders gasped with outrage and turned upon Mycroft with shouts and stares. Meanwhile, dodging between skirts and ducking beneath gentlemanly elbows, I took refuge once more in the Ladies' Lavatory, whisking past the doorkeeper with a gabbled tale of having forgotten something. Hurrying straight into that excellent facility's inner sanctum, I found the maidservant at work with her perfume-atomiser, attempting to quell the inevitable stench.

"Vanish," I snapped at her, and without a murmur she retreated to the parlour.

By the time Mycroft had, I surmise, explained himself and summoned a constable, I was gone through the back window, and I was no longer a female scholar. Minus hat, gloves, and glasses, I no longer resembled that drab creature at all, thanks to a colourful length of Indian-print cotton—I always carry such useful things in my bust, for emergencies and also to lend me the appearance of the bosom I do not possess. Thus, looking quite the Bohemian with my bare hands, my head wrapped like that of a heathen and my shawl trailing halfway to the ground, I walked to the Underground and made my way safely back to "Dr. Ragostin's" office.

None of the servants saw me come in, for I did not, in my outlandish costume, enter by the front door. Rather, I pressed the centre of a certain scroll amid the wood ornamentation that dripped like cake-sugar all over the house's gingerbread-brown stone façade, then slipped around the side, opened the secret door, and strode directly into the locked inner room, "Dr. Ragostin's" private office. It was my very good fortune that this sanctum had been fitted out for use by a medium (a villain—but that is another story) who had once held séances there—hence the secret door, behind a bookshelf, to the outside, and also a small secret chamber where I kept my various disguises.

I threw my Bohemian shawl aside, turned up the gas-lamps for light, then lounged upon the chintz sofa, frowning.

Angry at myself. Had I been alert and taking proper precautions, looking about me, the encounter with Mycroft would never have happened. Now, in addition to embarrassing myself (I was not yet ready to rejoice in the way I had embarrassed *him*), I had lost my chance to shadow Lady Cecily and find out what mysterious new misfortune might beset her. Even the number of the cab she had taken was lost from my mind, which apparently had dropped it during the fracas. I was left with no clue except the peculiar fan lying in my lap. Indeed, if it were not for that candy-pink artefact, I would have found it difficult to believe what had happened.

Holding the fan up to the light, I scanned it.

Then, pulling a magnifying-lens from my bosom, I studied it inch by inch. I hoped to find a note or message, but discovered only plain sticks, their cheap soft wood unmarred by any scratched or pencilled lines, and plain pink paper, slightly watermarked in a decorative checkerboard motif, but quite virginal. As was the fan's edging of downy feathers, no doubt plucked from some common backyard duck before being dyed pink. I could see no marks on the shafts of the feathers, nothing slipped between sticks and paper, no hidden compartment, simply nothing of interest.

Confound it all. If only—

Drat Mycroft. Drat and blast brothers.

Grumpily I moved to "Dr. Ragostin's" vast mahogany desk, where, with pencil and drawing paper, I sketched quite an alarming picture of Mycroft at the moment he had recognised me, his bushy brows all shot up as if he had just trod upon a rat. Then, my feelings somewhat relieved, more contemplatively I drew a likeness of Lady Cecily in her bell skirt. Often when I find myself in doubt, upset, or perplexity, I turn to sketching, and I generally find that it does good somehow.

In no way is Lady Cecily a fool for fashion. Why ever would she wear a bell skirt?

Doodling, I remembered the flat boater I had seen on her head.

Why such a frightfully modish costume, yet a hat not the least bit fashionable?

Next I started sketching her face, first in profile, then from the front.

The style in which she wore her hair, pulled straight back, was not fashionable, either. If she cared about fashion, she would have worn a fringe to cover that high forehead. Why, she looks a bit like Alice in Wonderland. Despite Sir John Tenniel's marvelous illustrations, I had never much enjoyed Lewis Carroll's books.

Alice never smiled.

I did not like nonsense stories; I wanted narrative to unfold with some degree of logic, much as life should. Although often it did not. For instance, it made no sense that such a well-to-do girl as Lady Cecily should carry a paper fan.

Why such a silly pink thing?

Well and truly engrossed in my drawing now, I sketched Cecily again, this time putting the fan in her hand, and trying to capture the way she had looked at me —

With a shudder as if a whip had snapped far too close to me, I felt again the desperation of her gaze.

Something is dreadfully wrong.

Even though I did not at all understand what she wanted of me, I knew I must try to help her.

But how to find out what was the matter?

After a few moments' thought, I got up and strode

to a certain bookcase, where I reached behind a stout volume of Pope's essays and touched a hidden latch. Quite silently the shelf turned upon its well-oiled hinges, allowing me passage into my very private "dressing-room," where I began to affect necessary changes in my costume and appearance.

I had decided to go calling upon the Alistairs. Therefore, because Lady Theodora knew me only as the mousy Mrs. Ragostin, I must once again become that humble person.

Timid, fumbling, and dowdy even though she carried a lorgnette and a parasol, "Dr. Ragostin's" child bride (remembering to tap softly) plied the brass knocker upon the formidable front door of the baronet's town house. I had achieved the dowdiness by combining grey cotton gloves and quite a limp olive-green felt hat with an expensive but hideous brown print dress. Moreover, I had tucked moss-roses, an old-fashioned blossom, into my hatband and my bosom. (Upper-class bosoms are expected to serve as flowerpots.) I hoped Lady Theodora would see me; from my previous visits I knew that she, a radiantly beautiful woman, found Mrs. Ragostin, who was quite the opposite, soothing to her nerves.

But when the redoubtable butler answered the door, he bore no silver tray, nor did he so much as glance at the calling-card in my gloved hand, although I am sure he recognised me. "Lady Theodora is receiving no visitors."

"Her ladyship is unwell?" I ventured, remembering to keep my tone that of a well-bred sparrow.

"Her ladyship is seeing *no one*."

Hmm. If it were an ordinary matter of indisposition, he would have agreed that her ladyship was unwell.

"Tomorrow, perhaps?" I chirped.

"Most unlikely. Her ladyship remains in total seclusion."

Another baby on the way, perhaps? As if poor Theodora had not borne enough little Alistairs already? She must be of an age to cease. Was this mysterious seclusion mere coincidence, or did it have something to do with Lady Theodora's most problematic daughter?

Displaying distress or vacuity of mind, I began to twitter. "How very disappointing. Since I am here . . . I have been quite wanting to meet . . . might I have just a word with Lady Cecily?"

"The Honourable Lady Cecily no longer resides here."

This surprised me, for two reasons: where was Cecily if not here, at her home? And why had the butler been so frank? I saw by his sour expression that already he regretted his indiscretion; evidently my persistent brown presence was wearing him down.

Encouraged, I did not budge from the doorstep. "Really! Lady Cecily has gone already to the country, perhaps?"

But I was to get nothing more out of him. Excusing himself, he shut the door in my face.

So much for talking with Lady Theodora.

Now what?

Chapter
the
Third

THAT EVENING, IN MY CUSTOMARY GUISE AS DR. Ragostin's secretary, Ivy Meshle, I went home to my rented lodging and shared a less-than-satisfactory supper of carrots and kidneys with my elderly landlady. Since Mrs. Tupper is as deaf as a cast-iron gatepost, I attempted no conversation while we ate. But afterward, I signalled her that I wished to borrow some reading material from her. That is to say, I spread my hands as if opening a newspaper, then pointed upward, towards her bedchamber. There were only three rooms in her East End hovel: mine, hers, and the single cooking/dining/sitting-room on the ground floor. Still, the sweet old soul did not understand. Placing her trumpet to her ear, she leaned towards me over the table and bellowed, "What? You say there's a bat got in upstairs?"

Eventually I had to lead her upstairs to show her what I wanted: her stacks of society periodicals.

As a step towards finding and helping Lady Cecily, I hoped to discover the identity of the ogresses in whose dubious company I had seen her.

Society-watching was a pursuit that, being a person of democratic convictions, I had scorned, up until now. So I had a great deal of catching up to do. After carrying Mrs. Tupper's accumulated periodicals to my own room, gladly I rid myself not only of my dress but my bust enhancer, hip regulators, and corset, my cheek and nostril inserts, my fringe of curls, and my false eyelashes, making myself comfortable in a dressing-gown and slippers before settling down to read.

Although I cannot say I particularly enjoyed it. Over the course of the next several hours I learned that croquet was quite passé, tennis and archery still in mode, but the Very Latest Sport for ladies was golf. Lord Jug-ears and Lady Parsnip-face had been seen coaching in Hyde Park; she wore a Worth gown of ciel-bleu French gibberish moire. What a shame that Kensington Palace stood empty despite its restoration. A most distinguished gathering had attended the christening of Baby So-and-so, firstborn son of Lord Such-a-much Earl of What-does-it-matter. Satin was Out, *peau de soie* In. An oil-painting exhibition themed around the Progress of the British Empire was viewable at Gallery Ever-so-exclusive. Viscount and Viscountess Ancient-lineage announced the engagement of their daughter Long-name to Great-prospects, the younger son of Earl Blue-blood. My head ached abominably, I thought I should go quite mad, and I had not yet looked through even a quarter of the stack. I peered at photographs of Duchess Duck-foot's boating-party, Baron Bulb-nose's cricket-team's annual banquet, Debutante Wasp-waist's coming-out ball, and dozens more without finding either of the two unpleasant faces I sought.

When day turned to dark, gladly I rose from my chair, for I would strain my eyes if I attempted to read any longer by candlelight. From its hiding place between mattress and bedstead I pulled the dark, decrepit clothing I wore when I went out to wander the night.

Now that winter had passed, poor folk living in the streets were less in need of my help. And since my brother Sherlock knew of my work as the Sister of Charity, I had been obliged to discard my black habit with deep pockets. While I still managed to slip pennies to the unfortunate, I had found another guise in which to roam London in the dark hours: I went as a midden-picker, that is, one who scavenges garbage heaps for bits of rag (for the paper-mills), bone (for garden-meal), metal (for the smelters), or food (definitely not for me). I wore a shabby skirt and shawl, walked with a rickety, shambling gait, and carried a battered lantern in one hand and a burlap sack upon my bent back.

Some innate unrest drives me to roam the night in any event, but in settling upon this particular guise, I gave myself a purpose: I wanted to learn my way around all of London, not just the East End. As a midden-picker, I could go anywhere without interference, for I exemplified thriftiness. Although propriety dictated that such an unsightly scavenger must steal in and out again by night, still, only the most mean and stingy of households would drive such a hardworking representative of the "deserving poor" from their premises.

Whether Mrs. Tupper was asleep yet or not, there was no fear that the dear deaf soul would hear me go out. Latching the door behind me, I made my way into the crowded street—in the warm months, the narrow lanes of the slums thronged even at midnight. Arm in arm, a clot of men staggered past, singing a drunken song. On one corner by the light of a street-lamp, haggard women sewed sacks for flour and such, piecework to bring in a few farthings, until their hands and eyes could labour no more. On another corner loitered other women, showing a great deal of bosom and ankle, also at work but not sewing. Everywhere children meandered aimlessly. It sometimes seemed to me that half the population of London was children, and half the children were orphans—it was very much the usual thing for a girl of the slums to have a baby by the time she was fifteen, then die in her twenties—whilst the other half were "Hansels and Gretels," turned out by parents who could not feed them.

This was East London. Ten minutes on the Underground took me to West London, which might as well have been a different world.

Especially the neighbourhood where I went that night. Here, square old houses slept, blanketed in ivy, surrounded by square fenced yards. Here, streets ran wide and empty into yet more squares—cobbled squares. This area was like a great square-patch brick-and-stone quilt I had not yet comprehended to my satisfaction; what sort of people lived here? In a square-towered Italianate villa, nouveau riche or impoverished royalty? In a mansard-roofed French Second Empire edifice, maiden aunts or dilettantes? In a much-gabled Queen Anne, a doctor? A dandy?

Gas lighted some of the houses; others stood dark. Ambling along, I saw no one except a pair of night-soil men making their rounds—while there might be water-closets within the houses, there were still back-garden privies that needed to be emptied, and this distasteful process had to be done by darkness. Hence the men with the great metal container on a cart. After the rumble of its wheels had faded away (although its fetor, alas, had not), I saw and heard no other persons—except, coming towards me, the measured pacing of a constable on his beat.

"Gud evenin', ducks," I piped as he approached me.

"And many gud evenin's to yerself, dearie." He was Irish and cheery, twirling his baton, nodding approval of my burlap sack. "Me nose was tellin' me, afore them stinkers passed, that it's mock turtle soup they're afther havin' at number forty-four."

"Thank ye kindly." Off I scuttled, lighting my sorry little lantern, and sure enough, in back of number forty-four I found the skull of the calf's head they had boiled.

One can hypothesise about people by their midden-heaps. For instance: perhaps members of this household had aspirations that exceeded their means, as turtle soup, the genuine item, was all the rage among the rich.

Once behind the houses, with the calf's skull in my bag and the constable's friendliness bolstering my nerve, I zigzagged from backyard to backyard, entering mostly through carriage-drives; from each carriage-house a dog would bark in a perfunctory manner, to be shushed by the boy or groom sleeping in the loft overhead after he had taken a peep at me through his window. Thus admitted to the nether-world of the neighbourhood, I started to sort out the inhabitants in my mind. Sometimes there were veg-etable gardens tucked behind the carriage-houses where they could easily be enriched by manure and straw: solid and sensible folk, these. Some houses seemed empty, perhaps waiting for an owner to re-turn from abroad, but quite a few were occupied by families with children, as evidenced by hoops, brightly striped balls, clapping-monkey pull-toys, et cetera, left lying about. And someone had a seamstress living in, sewing the entire family new springtime outfits, for in the midden-heap I found threads and scraps of everything from serge to taffeta—all of which I bagged by the light of my lantern.

But at the next house, I saw as I shuffled towards its back fence, I needed no lantern. For some rea-son these people kept gas-jets flaring out-of-doors, like a modern sort of flambeau. How wasteful, and how odd.

The gate to the carriage-drive was padlocked. But through the iron rails of the fence, and by the light of all those outdoor gas-jets, I could see quite a pile of bones just past the corner of the carriage-house.

Once one begins collecting something, for whatever reason, the act becomes a sort of mania in itself. Even though, at the night's end, I would give away my finds to the first beggar I encountered, nevertheless, when I saw those bones, I had to have them. Forgetting that I was supposed to be a bent and rickety woman of the slums, I swarmed up and over the fence within a moment; I love to climb, and seldom get the chance, as this is not a pastime much pursued by proper females. Lighthearted as well as light-footed, I jumped down inside the fence and turned towards my objective.

But I'd not gone three steps when a roar worthy of a Bengal tiger paralysed me. A huge animal charged me, bearing down on me like a galloping horse.

Ye gods! I had not seen the doghouse tucked behind the carriage-house, and now the proper owner of the bones—a massive mastiff—wished to tear my throat out.

With no time to retreat over the fence, I was in a panic, fumbling for my dagger, when, quite unexpectedly, the beast halted, although it continued to roar and snarl at me in the most resounding and frightful manner.

What ever in the world? Why was I not being mauled?

Then I saw.

Oh, my goodness.

The mastiff had halted on the far side of another, inner fence. But not the usual sort of fence. Unless I was much mistaken—

"What do you have there, Lucifer?" drawled an insolent voice, and a massive man, rather resembling his mastiff, appeared from between beech trees and walked up on the far side of the inner fence.

The sunk fence, so called. Also known as a ha-ha.

A deep ditch lined with stone. Such modern moats were not uncommon around country estates, hidden in the contours of the land so as to preserve the integrity of the vista whilst keeping out cattle and intruders—but here in the city? What ever for?

"A midden-picker," the burly man was saying with disgust, eyeing me as if I were a cockroach to be crushed. "How did you get in?"

Making myself as small as possible—not difficult, under the circumstances—I did not answer, only staring at the sunk fence with my mouth ajar.

"You don't know what it is, do you, bones-for-brains?" I could hear the man's sneer in his voice. "It's a ha-ha. And do you know why it's called that, dust-scholar? It's called that because, when you fall in, we come and look at you and we laugh, ha-ha, ha-ha—"

Something in the tone of his voice frightened me even more than the mastiff's barking did. I began to back away.

" —ha-ha, ha-ha —"

I dodged into the shadows behind the carriage-house, out of his view, and applied myself earnestly to climbing over the wrought-iron fence.

" —ha-ha, and then we go away," he shouted after me, "and leave you there until you rot!"

I was never in any danger, really. Yet, until I had got home again and lay safe in my bed, I could not stop trembling.

CHAPTER
THE
FOURTH

THE NEXT MORNING, REPORTING TO THE STEEP-gabled and fancifully ornamented Gothic house where "Dr. Ragostin" maintained his office, I carried quite a load of "society papers" in my arms.

"Good morning, Miss Meshle!" cried my irrepressible page-boy, holding the door open for me.

"If you say so, Joddy." Going indoors felt grim despite the May sunshine streaming through the chintz curtains. I felt still shadowed by last night's odd encounter. But it scarcely mattered, compared to the problem of the peculiar pink fan. Just as my reading material burdened my arms, the mystery surrounding Lady Cecily burdened my mind. Why had she so cleverly slipped to me her paper "toy," of which I could make nothing?

Sighing, I sent Joddy for newspapers, rang for

tea, then settled at my desk with the Grub Street periodicals to enrich my knowledge of society some more. Lord Globe-trotter will address the Ladies of Inanity on the topic of his recent voyage down the Nile . . . The Honourable Miss Disapproval breaks her engagement to The Honourable Mr. Disappointment . . . To soften and beautify the hair, beat up the whites of four eggs into a froth, rub it into the roots, and leave it there . . . New for spring, the bias-cut invisible-seamed wrap morning-dress . . . *I truly shall go mad* . . . Colour-themed entertaining the latest rage; the yellow luncheon, the pink —

Wait a moment.

The Pink Tea, just now so fashionable, is an expensive way of entertaining; yet one might as well be dead as out of fashion! So here is how a true Pink Tea should be done: The table linen should be pink, the dishes also of a delicate pink shade, which you may borrow for the occasion. Arrange white cakes on high cake-stands lined with fancy pink paper, and pink frosted cakes on low cake-stands lined with fancy white paper. The table should be illuminated with a chandelier of pink candles; flowers for decoration must also be of pink, and your maids should wear pink caps and pink aprons. Serve the creams and ices in novel designs made of pink paper, such as baskets, bandboxes, seashells, or wheelbarrows. These along with

party favours in many more beautiful designs may be procured at any fashionable caterer's . . .

Paper party favours.

Pink.

Including, perhaps, cheap pink fans?

A connection, a thread, a very thin thread indeed, but better than nothing.

Sitting up quite straight, I rang the bell, and when, in Joddy's absence, the kitchen-maid appeared, I asked her to convey to Mrs. Bailey and Mrs. Fitzsimmons my request that they might kindly favour me with their presence for a moment.

I should explain that in "Dr. Ragostin's" Gothic establishment there was not merely an office to be looked after, but a house full of boarders (to stabilise my finances), for all of which Mrs. Fitzsimmons served as housekeeper, Mrs. Bailey as cook.

Those two doughty white-capped women appeared before me with the same doubtful expression on each dumpling-cheeked face. After months in "Dr. Ragostin's" employ without ever having seen the man, surely they suspected that I was something more than a mere secretary.

After greeting them pleasantly enough—although I did not invite them to sit down—I asked, "Where might one find such a thing as a caterer?"

Mrs. Bailey puffed up like a ruffled hedgehog. "What would yer want a caterer fer? I can do anythin'—"

But before the offended cook could further defend her territorial right to her kitchen, I silenced her. "I simply asked, where are caterers to be found?"

In what area of London, I meant. Just as birds of a feather flock together, so did businesses in that city: bankers on Threadneedle Street, tailors on Savile Row, sixpenny magazines on Grub Street, physicians on Harley, dead fish principally at Billingsgate Market.

After an interval of discussion, Mrs. Fitzsimmons and Mrs. Bailey agreed that most of the caterers were to be found near Gillyglade Court, an offshoot of the fashionable shopping district around Regent Street.

An hour or so later, a cab pulled up at a corner of that commercial mecca and quite a well-bred young lady descended: yours truly. In order to transform myself, I had made use of my secret dressing-room, where I had removed rouge, cheek and nostril inserts, false eyelashes, hair additions, et cetera, but then crowned my own narrow, sallow, aristocratic face with the most gloriously coiffed wig, to which I attached a hat consisting mostly of a pouf of feathers and lace. Next, touches of perfume and powder, then a perfectly divine promenade dress of celadon-green dotted swiss with the very latest in puffed sleeves, also dove-grey kid-leather boots and gloves, a white organza parasol, and voila! Impeccably upper-class, with my dagger as always sheathed in the bust of my corset, but now concealed by a handsome opal brooch.

Regent Street and its environs can be summed up in three words: *glass, gas,* and *brass.* That is to say, oft-cleaned bow windows replete with finery illuminated by numerous lamps in the most resplendent of all possible surroundings. On this fine day, polished door-knobs and the like appeared even more shining than usual, because less sooty. With silk petticoats rustling beneath my trailing skirt I perambulated in and out of the glittering shops, twirling my parasol and smiling amiably and condescendingly upon clerks bobbing behind the counters. After a brief while, my seemingly aimless peregrinations carried me into Gillyglade Court.

At each door I entered, my posh clothing plus my aristocratic accent drew instant servility from clerks. I quickly located several caterers and learned more than I wanted to know about their services. I could have rented burnished silver Persian coffee-urns, pressed-glass plates, potted ferns, showy epergnes — sublimely useless — for the centre of each table, or golden birdcages complete with nightingales to hang from the ceiling; I was offered seven-course menus, wine-lists, a selection of "refections" including but certainly not limited to bonbons with humourous mottoes folded into them upon slips of paper.

Indeed, these caterers could do almost anything with paper.

"I have heard that a pink-themed tea is quite the thing for spring," I said at each of five establishments, gazing vaguely around me through my lorgnette.

And at each the response was much the same. "Oh! Yes, yes indeed," and I would be shown a plethora of pink gimcracks: pink doilies, pink daisies, pink paper sailboat candy-holders, pink paper rose-petal bowls, pink paper squirrels, top-hats, mushrooms, camels, pyramids . . .

All of which I would regard with slight but evident revulsion as I said doubtfully, "I don't know . . . something a bit more elegant . . . have you any fans?"

No. No, alas, they did not.

But at the sixth caterer's shop, they did.

"Oh! Oh, yes, we made them up special for the Viscountess of Inglethorpe, and they were a great success, so we made some more to keep on hand; just a moment and I will fetch one to show you."

And out came the pink paper fan.

Seemingly identical in every detail to the one the girl in the bell skirt had slipped to me.

"Let me see that," I demanded, retaining my imperial manner but quite forgetting my pose of indifference as I grabbed the pink paper fan and held it up to the light, peering at it, nay, glaring at it through my lorgnette, for something was wrong. Different. "Is this the same paper you used for, ah—"

"For the Viscountess of Inglethorpe? Yes, exactly the same."

Good-quality heavy pink paper, but plain. No watermark of any kind.

I stood there a moment, and I am sure the hapless clerk must have wondered why I scowled so.

"May I take this with me?" I daresay I sounded angry, although my exasperation was all for myself.

"Of course."

"Thank you." Ungraciously I stormed out, muttering to myself as I strode towards the nearest cab-stand, "Blind. I have been *blind*."

How could I have overlooked a device so simple and obvious?

Humph. I had been dense. Obtuse. *Stupid*. But knowing what I did now, with my finger upon the right clue at last, I felt sure that I would soon learn the nature of Lady Cecily's difficulty.

CHAPTER
THE
FIFTH

MISS MESHLE RETURNED TO HER LODGING MUCH earlier than usual that day, attempting and failing to give a smiling greeting to the startled Mrs. Tupper and her equally startled girl-of-all-work.

Blessedly, the deafness of the former and the humble status of the latter rendered any explanation unnecessary. I simply nodded, waved, and strode upstairs. The moment I had closed and locked the door of my room behind me, I pounced upon the peculiar pink fan Lady Cecily had slipped to me. Holding it up to the window, I studied once more the faint markings upon the pink paper.

Markings I had taken for a sort of checkered decorative motif, a watermark.

And I confess that I said something quite naughty,

for I should have guessed the first moment I saw them.

But vexation would get me nowhere. Mentally setting emotion aside, I struck a match, with which I lit a sconce of candles. Then, taking my pink mystery in hand once more, I opened it until it formed a nearly flat half-circle, and began gently to warm it at the flames, careful not to scorch the paper.

Gingerly moving it about to heat all portions of it equally and slowly, I watched brown lines beginning to emerge from the background of pink.

Yes.

Invisible writing.

I noted with approval that Lady Cecily, with the instinct of a true artist, must have used a tiny brush rather than a pen, to leave no impressions upon the paper itself after her "invisible ink"—most likely lemon juice—had dried.

My heartbeat hastened, for the secret message written on the fan was almost ready to be read.

Rather, deciphered.

When I felt sure the fan's pink paper had yielded all the brown lines that it was likely to show me, I hurried to sit down with my writing desk in my lap, snatched up some foolscap paper, and began to copy the missive in pencil in case the original might fade. Even now it was difficult to see clearly. With some guesswork I transcribed it thus:

45

Several weeks earlier, during a period of inactivity and, I must confess, loneliness, I had obtained and read a publication upon the subject of secret writing and ciphers. Not something I would normally pick up, but this particular "trifling monograph" (his own words) had been authored by Sherlock Holmes, my brother; I had read and reread it just to "hear" his precise and coolly passionate voice.

Thanks to Sherlock, then, I knew that what I saw before me was called the "Mason" cipher, having been invented by Freemasons in the past century — but I could easily have solved it even before having read my brother's excellent text, for this "secret code" was no secret, being commonly used among schoolchildren everywhere. Indeed, it could be decoded so simply that I wondered why Lady Cecily had bothered to use a cipher at all.

At the top of my paper I scrawled the key:

To encipher from this, one drew the shape of each letter's container, so to speak. Absurdly simple. Deciphering was just as easy. Referring back to the secret message, I quickly translated it, thus:

HELCLOCKEDIA
EBBMFGAEIED
UNLES

That was all.

"Curses," I grumbled, glaring at the less-than-satisfactory message before me. The only words that made any sense were *clock* and, at the end, *unless*, misspelled.

"Unless"? Unless what? The word suggested altercation. Do such-and-so unless you want a thrashing, or won't do such-and-so unless . . .

Unless what? A sentence ought not to end with *unless*.

Unless the word were not misspelled, but incomplete? The message had been interrupted? Suggesting duress?

I felt in my bones that I had hit upon the truth; Lady Cecily had been unable to finish her message. Evidently she was closely watched. I wished she had simply written in plain English, for she could have managed that more quickly.

But then I realised why she had not done so. "Invisible" ink, although it dries clear, is not actually impossible to see; it leaves a sheen noticeable in certain lights. Handwriting might have been detected. But the straight-lined cipher had concealed itself nicely along the folds of the fan, looking like a sort of decoration, while being simple for a recipient to solve.

Clever.

And desperate. A cipher secretly written in invisible ink on a paper fan of all things, then slipped to someone she met by accident, someone she barely knew — certainly such a cipher ought to be a plea for assistance, for rescue, for help —

Of course.

The first four letters were not *HELC*; they were *HELP*. The cipher for *P* looked just like the cipher for *C* except that it included a dot, which evidently I had not perceived.

What of *clock*, then?

Eureka! The next word had to be *locked*!

Feverishly addressing my pencil to the cipher again, mindful of missing dots, I eventually arrived at the following:

Deciphered:

HELPLOCKEDIN
ROOMSTARVED
UNLES

Or, in plainer English, "Help! I am being locked in my room and starved — unless . . ."

I must admit that my first reaction upon reading this was one of immense gratification; I felt all of the thrill of the chase. And of elucidation: Eureka! I understood why Lady Cecily had worn such a silly thing as a bell skirt. She had been forced to do so, in order to hobble her so that she could not possibly run away from her dragonish chaperones. Now, with her errands completed, she was, presumably, locked away again. But where? Here was a case of a missing person indeed! I anticipated search, adventure, perhaps even a rescue —

But immediately my fervour turned to horror for Cecily's sake. Could I find her in time? Could I find her before —

What? She was being locked up and starved unless what?

Unless she yielded to some demand, obviously. Unless she obeyed some command she had so far defied. Unless she agreed to —

"Oh, no," I whispered as I remembered. "Oh, how awful! Could it be?"

A trousseau you will need, and a trousseau you shall have, one of the guardian dowagers had said.

I had no very clear idea what a trousseau looked like or what might be included in one; to the best of my knowledge it consisted of expensive, lacy unmentionables. But I knew what a trousseau was *for*.

They had brought her to London to shop for a trousseau.

This meant that there was none prepared already—there had been no period of engagement during which ribbons and ruffles might lovingly be stitched—and there was no time to order a supremely fashionable one from abroad.

In my horror I leapt to my feet, spilling paper, pencil, and writing desk to the floor.

Lady Cecily was going to be married.

Soon.

And against her will.

CHAPTER THE SIXTH

I HAD TO FIND HER. HAD TO FIND LADY CECILY AND rescue her from such a dreadful and unjust fate.

But how?

Enola, calm yourself. Think. That voice from within—it was as if my mother spoke to me, and for a moment Mum's face filled my mind.

A comforting memory, but with it came a discomfiting thought: I had been putting off the task of finding Mum. Why?

Did I really not wish to see her?

What sort of daughter was I?

But then again, it was Mum who had first run away, not I.

Yet hadn't I forgiven her?

Blast everything! Confound questions I could not answer—no, did not wish to answer.

Mentally thrusting them to the side, I sat down, picked up pencil and paper again, and told myself that, being in such dire straits, Lady Cecily came foremost. Then Mum. Then, a distant third, the Army general's leg-bone, which, after all, he no longer needed for any practical purpose.

Regarding Lady Cecily, what concerning her difficulty did I know surely?

Next to nothing.

Very well; what could I surmise?

I wrote:

Her mother is in seclusion

I cannot imagine Lady Theodora favouring forced marriage

Lady Cecily has been taken away from her mother

Probably Sir Eustace's idea

Which made sense. What to do with an unconventional, politically opinionated, distressingly left-handed daughter who has been scandalously kidnapped and will therefore be considered spoilt goods upon the marriage market? Why, bypass the usual coming-out by arranging some private disposal of the girl, probably by financial inducement.

It appeared that the two dragons with whom I had seen Cecily had charge of her for the time being. My task now was to identify and locate them.

I wrote,

Her chaperones, proud and richly clothed, seem to be of noble blood

The chaperones seemed to wield familial authority over her

They dressed her in greenish yellow; might they be of Aesthetic taste?

Cecily and her entourage took a cab, number _____

She most likely got the fan attending a pink tea —the Viscountess of Inglethorpe's pink tea?

All in all, not very helpful.

Although I could not remember the number of the cab, still, I decided, I could be moderately proud of myself for having remembered the name of the viscountess.

Indeed, it was my only clue.

If any of the society papers might, perhaps, have

run a little "piece" about her pink tea party and . . .
supposing that the chaperones had attended along
with Lady Cecily . . . if I could find an account that
listed the names of the guests . . .

But as my eyes turned towards the pile of rub-
bish I would have to read, I groaned aloud. Even if
I found what I was looking for, then it would be
necessary for me somehow to sort through the guests
in order to find Lady Cecily's ogresses-in-waiting.
Or even worse, what if I scanned the confounded
papers for hours and hours and, after all, the viscountess's blasted tea party were not even *there*? A
viscountess was not, after all, the social equal of a
duke's wife or even an earl's; what if no society reporter had bothered to—

An idea caught hold with such force that my
breath snagged in my throat. I let it stay there for a
moment as I considered. Then, breathing out, I
smiled.

While I had no actual knowledge of what a society
reporter might be like, I could imagine: a female
with more education than means, a genteel miss
rather like a governess, obliged to make a living until
she found a man to take care of her. Her clothing
might be plain, even threadworn, but never lacking
in taste. An object of kindness and condescension.

In great haste I began to hunt up my very proper,

all-purpose brown tweed suit. Because I had skipped luncheon, there would still be time today.

An hour or so later, in the aforementioned well-worn suit, neatly gloved and hiding beneath a brown hat's veil, with a stenographer's notebook and a bundle of pencils in hand, I presented myself at the door of the Viscount of Inglethorpe's city residence.

To the oversized tin soldier of a butler who eventually answered my knock, I said, "I am from the *Women's Gazette*." I had checked many back issues of this much-admired publication, found no mention of anything Inglethorpe, and felt myself to be treading on fairly safe ground as I went on. "They have sent me to see whether I might do a feature on the viscountess's pink tea."

"A bit late, aren't you?" rumbled the butler. "That was over a week ago."

When in doubt, say nothing. I replied only with a meek smile.

His brows drew together. "Don't you have a card?"

"I'm new," I improvised. "They haven't printed me one yet."

"Oh, so that's the way it is. They send out a novice a week late." I did not mind the resentment in his tone, for it showed that I had guessed rightly: the Viscountess of Inglethorpe quite wanted to be included in the society papers with the same frequency and scope as, for instance, a duchess; the viscountess felt herself much neglected in the ladies' press, and her household, naturally, shared this sentiment.

I repressed a smile, feeling sure now that I would be admitted; such vanity could not turn me away.

Indeed, even as the butler betook himself upstairs to consult with Lady Inglethorpe, already the housekeeper, an unexpectedly pleasant woman named Dawson, was showing me into the morning-room where the tea had taken place.

"We've left it just so," she was saying, "except for the flowers, of course, until the room is needed for something else, for my lady took great pains over the effect and likes to admire it."

Admire was perhaps not the word I would have used, for I felt as if I had stepped into a cow's udder. Never before had I entertained any prejudice against the colour pink, but I began to loathe it in that moment as I stood beneath pink-draped windows with pink lambrequins, tables swaddled in pink, walls—

Recollecting my guise, and also in order to hide my face in case it showed a touch of nausea, I flipped open a notebook and began feverishly to take notes: pink grosgrain ribbon swags on dado and pictures, pink net billowing down from the ceiling, pink Japanese lanterns dangling from pink crocheted strings.

"We served coconut cakes iced pink and white,

and we put pink ices shaped like cupids and swans on the tables. Her ladyship wore a pink tea-frock that come all the way from France, and us servants had pink caps and pink aprons made special for the occasion. Oh, with the pink candles and all, it was like a pink fairy-land in here!"

Clenching my teeth against any heartfelt retort, scribbling, I muttered, "Flowers?"

"Oh! The most lovely masses of pink cabbage roses, and for the gentlemen's buttonholes, pinks, only they were white—the flowers might be any co-lour but they are called 'pinks,' you know."

"Yes, I see." I forced a smile. "How witty."

"Her ladyship's idea. And for favours, there were pink paper fans for the ladies, and pink paper top-hats for the gentlemen."

Hollowly I responded, "How very amusing."

"Yes, great fun they had with them."

Finally, a chance at the information I wanted. "And the guests were?"

"Jacobs has gone to ask the viscountess whether he might give a copy of the guest list to you. Shall we go see whether he has come down?"

"Please." I am sure my tone sounded a bit too fervid; being in that room made me feel as if I had gorged upon sugar-plums. I drew a deep and thank-ful breath as we walked back into the more normally embellished hallway of the mansion.

But as we passed the drawing-room door, which stood open, I jolted to an abrupt halt, staring.

"Splendid, isn't it?" the housekeeper remarked when she realised what had distracted my attention.

At the far end of the formal room, in the place of honour over the mantel of the hearth, hung a large gold-framed oil portrait of a lady elegantly bestowed upon a fainting-sofa, a head-to-toe and nearly life-sized rendition of her carelessly holding a white Persian cat upon the most elaborate crimson figured-silk gown I had ever imagined or seen. Let me remark, as an aside, that the idea of keeping a house-cat in a mansion full of expensive china has always struck me as absurd, but it seems that the richer one is, the more one must show off such idiotic behaviour as endangering one's Waterford crystal, or clutching to one's bosom a creature guaranteed to rub white fur all over one's sable ruche. However, it was not any of these considerations, nor yet the remarkably in-full-fig costume of the woman in the portrait, that stopped my steps.

Rather, it was the dainty features of her fleshy face.

"That's my mistress, of course," the housekeeper was saying.

The viscountess: one of the matrons whom I had seen in the Ladies' Lavatory.

I had scarcely time to realise the peril in which I had placed myself before the butler's voice sounded behind me: "Lady Otelia Thoroughfinch, Viscountess of Inglethorpe, wishes to see you in her private sitting-room."

CHAPTER THE SEVENTH

OH.

The viscountess herself.

Oh, my. I felt an almost insurmountable urge to flee, as if somehow she knew—which of course she couldn't possibly—but what if she recognised me? And what if she then realised that I was not from the *Women's Gazette* at all, but was poking my rather pronounced nose into her affairs? What if she suspected I was in receipt of a peculiar pink fan—

All these frightened thoughts cried out in my mind even before I turned to follow the butler upstairs. At times such as these it is a very good thing that my father had been a logician, and I had educated myself with his books, as follows:

Premise: Viscountess Inglethorpe and I occupied the parlour of the Ladies' Lavatory at the same time.

Premise: She will recognise me.

Conclusion: Inconclusive.

Weak premise: She noticed me and recognises me.

Premise: She will realise I am NOT a reporter from the *Women's Gazette*.

Conclusion: Not valid, as such a reporter might very well use the Ladies' Lavatory.

However, just as these calming, rational thoughts began to take hold—also, just as I achieved the top of the stairway—there was a bang as the heavy front door whammed open, and a man's voice roared, "Ha-ha!"

I jumped and squeaked like a snared rabbit, for it was the voice of the exceedingly inhospitable man with the mastiff and the sunk fence!

But it couldn't be! my logical mind attempted once more to intercede. What possible reason—

"Ha-ha! Here we are!"

The butler, who in the expressionless way of butlers seemed as startled as I, said, "Excuse me just a moment, miss," and went downstairs again to see what was what, leaving me peering over the railing.

"File on in! Ha-ha! Gawk all you please, raga-muffins."

Oh, my evil stars, I could see now—it *was* the same burly man who had threatened to leave me rotting in his midnight ditch. Progressing into the entry hall resplendent in ascot, paddock-jacket, charcoal breeches, and cream-coloured gaiters, with his pugnacious face straining to maintain a smirk that was probably intended to be a smile, he was followed by a most unlikely company: orphans filing in two by two, little girls in the traditionally hideous brown gingham pinafores, with their hair cropped so short (for the prevention of lice) that they scarcely looked female despite their ruffled caps.

The butler approached the ha-ha man and bowed gravely, murmuring something.

"Just giving the little beggars a treat, ha-ha!" the man roared. From my refuge behind the stair railings I watched in fascination as his balding forehead turned tomato red. "Anything wrong with that?" The butler's deferential manner had apparently concealed some question of the man's presence under the circumstances.

"Look but don't touch," admonished a starchy middle-aged female at the end of the brown gingham line—a matron of the orphanage, I knew the instant I saw her, not merely because of her plain brown dress and her even more severe demeanour, but because she wore, like all such matrons, the most outlandish and unmistakable hat, white cotton starched into the shape of an inverted tulip with ruffles around its edge. The minute I had a chance, I must draw a picture of an orphanage matron like a plain brown tower with a bulbous white beacon on top.

"Shall I notify the viscountess?" the butler was asking. Or not asking, really. Warning.

"No need! Just showing the darlings what they have to look forward to, ha-ha! If they go into service in *my* house, you know, ha-ha!" With which outrageous statement—for quite plainly, from the butler's manner, this was not *his* house—the smirking and glowering mastiff-like man bellowed, "This way, urchins!" and strode onward. Huddled shoulder to shoulder, clutching each other's hands, with their faces displaying the terror I felt, the orphans followed more slowly. From behind, the matron herded them as they all disappeared from my view beneath the stairway from which I watched. Even though I knew that the ha-ha man had not seen me, and would not have recognised me in any event — even so, my heart thumped, and while ladies never sweat, or even perspire, certainly I felt my personage pass into the condition known as "all in a glow."

The butler returned upstairs, his white face so eloquently blank that I dared not ask him who the ha-ha man was. Indeed, I dared not speak.

With difficulty I made myself let go of the stair railing to which I had been clinging. In icy silence the butler showed me to a door. "Miss, um, the journalistic personage of whom I informed you, my lady," he announced me as he opened it. He intended, it seemed, to allow his mistress to remain ignorant of the invasion downstairs, at least for the moment and in my dubious presence.

"Yes. Quite." As the viscountess brusquely gestured for me to enter, she scarcely looked at me, thank goodness; after a moment I was able to take a deep breath and regain some measure of calm. Her ladyship did not, of course, invite me to be seated; a common news-reporter would not be staying long. Nor did she give me a chance to ask her any questions; she quite took charge. "I want you to see what I wore for the pink tea." On cue, a maid-in-waiting emerged from a walk-in closet, carrying a fabric confection of pink. "That is a Worth gown," the viscountess declared, and she began to read aloud from a salon program. "'This exquisite tea-gown is fashioned from pink chine pompadour taffeta with graceful godet pleating, trimmed around the—' Write it down! I want you to get it all just as I say."

Obediently I scribbled, meanwhile aware that

the jade damask at-home day-dress the viscountess wore might be described every bit as elaborately; indeed, it seemed to me one might almost be presented to the queen in it. It could not have been more apparent to me that this woman had aspirations above her station.

"'—trimmed around the neckline with puffed white tulle over scallops of pearl-studded sateen, while a double strand of rare pink pearls begins at the bust and drapes to the right side of the skirt, fastened there with a clasp of pink gold inspired by Michelangelo's sibyls of the Sistine Chapel'—have you got all that?"

"Yes, my lady," I lied. "And might I inquire the names of those who attended, my lady?" Now that I knew who the viscountess was, I wanted to find out who had been the other dragonish dowager accompanying her, with Lady Cecily, on the occasion when I had first encountered them. I hoped the other ogress's identity might be disclosed by the pink tea guest list.

"Oh! Yes, I have the list here. There was the Countess of Woodcrock, of course." (She said this in such a by-the-bye manner that I knew the countess was her prize catch for the event.) "Lady Dinah Woodcrock; Count Thaddeus was unfortunately unable to attend. And then there were the three daughters of the Earl of Throstlebine, the Honourable Misses Ermengarde, Ermentrude, and Ermenine Crowe, escorted by—"

This went on and on, until I began to despair of ever sorting it out.

". . . and the Baroness Merganser. Lady Aquilla Merganser. She is my sister, you know."

"Oh, really?" My interest was not feigned; did this sister by any chance look almost exactly like her? Was Lady Aquilla Merganser the one—

"Indeed. Aquilla married rather beneath her station, I fear." (Pompous nonsense, for, practically speaking, a baron is no better or worse a creature than a viscount.) "Her husband did not attend, but she brought along her son, Bramwell, and his fiancée, the Honourable Cecily Alistair."

Yes! Oh, yes! As one ogress was the viscountess, almost certainly the other ogress had to be her sister Aquilla, who had a son named Bramwell, who intended to marry the unfortunate Lady Cecily. Finding it very difficult to hide my excitement as I scrawled the names, I babbled, "A very attractive young lady, I am sure."

"She could be, if she would trouble herself. Quite spoilt, and rather a child, I fear." But then, abruptly, as if my interest in Lady Cecily caused her to close a door on further discourse, Lady Otelia turned her back—her derriere, I noticed, showed the effect of too much horseback riding on a sidesaddle, being visibly assymetrical, the right part higher than the left. With difficulty I suppressed a smile.

The viscountess gestured dismissal. "That is all."

"Yes, my lady." One must play one's part; I actually bobbed a sort of curtsey. "Thank you, my lady."

The butler waited to show me out, his demeanour now so upright as to be nearly martial. I wondered whether the apparently uninvited parade of orphans had yet left the premises. But I did not dare mention them, for I had a request to make. Once safely down the stairs, I asked whether I might speak with the housekeeper, Dawson, again.

"Just for a moment, to thank her for her helpfulness," I toadied.

With lofty indifference the butler assented. A few moments later, the friendly Dawson sat down in the servants' lounge with me. She was pleased to go over the pink tea's guest list with me in much greater detail than her mistress had done.

I will spare the gentle reader any account of the gossip that necessarily preceded what I wanted to know. I encouraged several minutes of "confidences" before I felt it safe to display curiosity regarding Viscountess Otelia and her sister Lady Aquilla.

"Oh, yes," declared the good Dawson, "as like as two peas in a pod, they are."

Eureka! I thought. Just as I had surmised, it must

have been Baroness Aquilla I had seen with Viscountess Otelia and Lady Cecily in the Ladies' Lavatory.

My poor left-handed lady! I suppressed an urge to shudder for her: As Bramwell Merganser, the groom-to-be, was Aquilla's son, then unless I could thwart her scheme, that "charming" woman would become poor Cecily's mother-in-law.

Although yearning to know more of the proposed wedding, I needed to proceed carefully with Dawson, so as not to arouse suspicion; even the most garrulous servant retains loyalty to her mistress. I made myself sit back in my chair across the tea-table from her. "Have they many children?" I asked, as this was the question that would most naturally arise next concerning the sisters Otelia and Aquilla. The propagation of numerous children, although a nuisance among the lower classes, was considered quite a virtue among the gentry, exemplified by Queen Victoria herself, who had produced nine.

"Sadly, my lady the viscountess has no living progeny," said Dawson with sympathy, yet at the same time a certain relish that the tragedy of child mortality, due to spotted fever and the like, was not confined to the lower classes. "And of Baroness Aquilla's five, only Bramwell has survived to adulthood. She has made rather a mama's boy of him, I fear," added Dawson pensively as she refilled our teacups.

Outwardly, I hope, I remained bland, but inwardly I bayed and panted, a hound hot on the scent. "Indeed? How old is he?"

"Nearly thirty, and still living at home, doing nothing on his own. And he appears to be likely to spend the rest of his life that way, for all that he's soon to be married."

"Yes, so I see!" Very natural, my curiosity, very innocent. "This Lady Cecily Alistair, who is she?"

"A cousin. Her father, Eustace Alistair, is Lady Aquilla's brother, and Lady Otelia's, of course."

Oh, dear. How odious. Yet there was nothing scandalous in the arrangement, for cousins marrying cousins is a common practice among blue-bloods, to keep property in the family. With the unintentional effect, according to Malthus, that each generation grows uglier than the last.

And marrying his daughter to his sister's son was exactly the sort of thing Sir Eustace *would* do. I remembered how his concern had been all for hushing up scandal, rather than for his daughter's safety, when Cecily had been kidnapped. After her return, I felt sure, he had regarded her not as a victim but as a disgrace. He had no concern for her sensibilities. In order to avoid any further embarrassment to himself, therefore, he had arranged to marry her off privately rather than have her presented at court. I wondered how much dowry he had paid to the Mergansers.

Dawson awaited my response. "Um, a good match," I ventured.

"Yes, indeed, a very good match it is."

All this time I had put off a fascinating but indelicate question: I quite wanted to know who the ha-ha man was—a gentleman, by his dress, perhaps even titled, with some connection to this household? Therefore, even though I knew otherwise, I asked, "Was it Sir Eustace, by any chance, who so kindly escorted the orphans—"

But I had reached the limits of Dawson's willingness to divulge. She responded only with gentle distress: "No, indeed, that was not Sir Eustace, and as for his bringing those—those dreadfully *common* children into this house unannounced . . . But it's not my place to say more. You'll excuse me, I'm sure."

CHAPTER THE EIGHTH

I RETURNED TO "DR. RAGOSTIN'S" OFFICE IN AN uncertain frame of mind. Poor Cecily, poor high-minded, artistic, free-spirited girl! I knew how she felt as the whole world, seemingly, attempted to break that spirit. I knew what it was like to be a young female utterly at the mercy of relatives and legal guardians, forced into obedience. Only my mother's cleverness had saved me.

How was I to save Lady Cecily?

After lighting the gas-lamps, I made immediately for the bookshelves and seized upon *Boyles*, one's indispensable guide to the aristocracy. Having had no luncheon made me cross and stubborn, so much so that I refused to go home for dinner; instead I sat down at once to look up "Inglethorpe" and "Merganser," then proceed onward to other references until eventually I pieced together a sequence of events.

The father of Eustace, Aquilla, and Otelia, I discovered, had been the merest baronet—Sir Dorian Alistair, Bt.—not a lord, not even a member of the peerage. Moreover, his means had been in no way equal to his aspirations. However, he and his wife had put on a good show when it came time to launch their two daughters into society, and both Otelia and Aquilla apparently had possessed sufficient beauty and charm (although I found this hard to imagine) to marry "up." Eustace, also, had done very well by marrying Lady Theodora.

Boyles took me no farther, but from my personal knowledge, having met Lady Theodora, apparently the heavens were to be blessed that Sir Eustace's children took after their mother, not their father.

I knew that Lady Cecily vehemently disagreed with her father's views of charity (he gave none), society (heights to be climbed), and a woman's place (obey).

I wondered how much Lady Cecily's cousin, whom she was being forced to marry, resembled her father.

How very unfair that such an innocent, intelligent, sensitive girl—Cecily would have given her shoes to a beggar—that such a young lady should have been, first, cursed with Sir Eustace for a father, then kidnapped by a conniving villain—and now, *now* locked in a room and starved—where?

Boyles gave me Baron Merganser's London address, and it seemed sensible to start looking there. At once.

One cannot always and forever be changing clothes, especially if one were to have a look at the Merganser residence while there was still some daylight; the brown tweed suit would *do*, I told myself firmly. It was dark enough, as were my grey stockings and brown boots. The only thing likely to give me away in the night was my white collar, which I could remove when it was time. Thinking along these lines, I delayed only to snatch up several potentially useful items, jamming them into a carpet-bag.

Swinging this, I hailed a cab, a four-wheeler. "To Oakley Street," I told the driver, "and then just drive slowly." While sighing over the fee the man named, I reminded myself that in his vehicle I could see without being seen.

A very good thing, as I am sure my jaw dropped to my collar-ruffle when I sighted the house.

Could I have mistaken the address? No; the numbers were quite clearly displayed upon the gatepost of the spiked wrought-iron fence which surrounded an ivy-shrouded mansion amid copper beeches, their spreading limbs and odd russet leaves shading the grounds. Yes, there had been beeches . . . but could I be confused in my recollection? I certainly hoped so; a couple of blocks farther on, signalling the driver to stop, I told him to turn around and drive slowly back again.

So that I could take another look.

Which, no happier than the first, confirmed what I wished not to be the case: Baron Merganser's London home — an exceedingly ugly "pointed Gothic" edifice of steeply gabled grey stone, very likely complete with gargoyles — was the selfsame place at which, as a midden-picker, I had encountered a large and unpleasant man, a quite ferocious mastiff, and — most peculiar — a sunk fence.

I now realized who that ha-ha man must be, having seen him today, expensively dressed although most incongruously consorting with orphans — a circumstance which failed to lessen my fear of him — in a location that could hardly be coincidental.

Turning matters over in my mind, I felt dreadfully weary, entertaining a strong desire to go home and rest.

Instead, I had the cab drive me towards Covent Garden, where at a busy corner I dismissed it. From a street vendor I purchased some biscuits and a lemonade, forcing myself to eat and drink as I considered what I might do next.

Then, after a bit of wandering I found a butcher's stall, where I bought a large soup-bone with plenty of tasty-looking meat and gristle on it.

This, I thought as I stowed it (well-wrapped in brown paper) in my now-bulging carpet-bag, would distract the mastiff while I climbed the fence.

As for crossing the ha-ha—well, I had learned my lesson a few weeks prior when I had found myself climbing the wall of a most precipitous house, nearly falling half a dozen times before I had made my way to the rooftop, which had proved to be no less treacherous, plummeting me through glass—but I digress. My point is that, after surviving this fiasco with nothing worse than a few cuts, I had purchased a goodly length of strong rope and promised myself that never again would I venture into any irregular situation without it. Indeed, its tidy coils nestled beneath the soup-bone in my carpet-bag.

With the rope I should be able to improvise some way to achieve the other side of the ha-ha.

After which—I tried to plan as I walked to the nearest Underground station and waited upon the platform for the train that was to take me back towards my fateful destination—after which all I needed to do was get into the house, evade detection, find Lady Cecily, release her from captivity, and bring her away with me?

Heaven help me.

Quite a bit later, when it seemed reasonable to think that folk were abed, after the house-windows had gone dim and the streets quiet except for the monotonous tread of the constable, I slipped up to a certain wrought-iron fence, beside the carriage-house this time. There I unwrapped the soup-bone from its brown paper and lobbed it into the Merganser yard through the bars, pleased to see it land just where I intended, in front of the doghouse. I expected that the mastiff would then come charging out and give a woof or two before he discovered his treat.

However, the dog did not bark; indeed, I saw no sign of him. As before, gas-jets ranged around the outside of the house lit up the environs—what a reckless expenditure!—and I waited several moments, expecting the dog to appear out of some shadow, but he did not.

Hmm.

Might he be sound asleep in his lair?

I mistrusted such good luck, but saw no alternative except to continue. Softly I made my way to the corner of the fence behind the carriage-house, where the friendly shadows gathered thickest, and there, hanging my carpet-bag from my belt and knotting my skirt above my knees, I climbed.

No stable-boy shouted as I let myself down the fence's inner side. No watchdog barked. No alarm of any kind sounded.

Rather than soothing my apprehensions, however, the silence worried me. It seemed too lucky. As if I might be entering a trap.

Yet I felt there was no choice but to go on.

And next, I had to find a way across the sunk fence.

Before moving out of the shadows, I got down close to the ground, because I knew, from my childhood experience of country life, that this was what poachers did in order to make themselves less likely to be seen when venturing across open expanses of forbidden land. Crawling, therefore, I crept towards the edge of the ditch, alert in every sense for any disturbance in the night. Even my skin and the roots of my hair seemed to hearken.

I heard the distant rumble of wheels and clop of hooves on cobbles, the equally distant creak of some privy door swinging on its hinges, and high overhead, beech leaves rustling in a light breeze. Nothing more.

Until a voice spoke from somewhere quite nearby, shocking me rigid.

In a pent whisper it said, "Confound the entire wretched business."

A man's voice.

"I shall be a laughingstock," he whispered on with the fervour of one who vocalises merely to rid himself of unruly emotion. "How could I fail to foresee a device so childishly simple?"

He spoke, I realised, from the depths of the ha-ha.

His was a voice I had heard before.

Somehow my body recognised it in advance of my mind, which still lacked proper function due to shock and terror. But my skin and my limbs felt no fear. Quite the opposite. They hurried me forward, still crawling, until I could look over the edge into the ditch.

Ten feet from me, at the bottom of that dark abyss, the midnight mutterer had lit a match in order to study his predicament, so I saw him clearly. He wore black clothing, a black cap, and he had darkened his face with soot, but I knew him readily enough.

My brother Sherlock.

CHAPTER
THE
NINTH

MY EMOTIONS MIGHT AS WELL HAVE BEEN A STAMPEDE of wild horses, they knocked me so witless. Yet, I must admit, one of my numerous feelings ran clearly and triumphantly in the fore: sheerest glee.

How the mighty had fallen.

The match-flame had travelled down the stick until it burned Sherlock's fingers. Dropping his light, he said something unrepeatable, and from the darkness above his head I told him, "Shame on you."

Even as the match went out, I saw him startle in a most satisfactory manner. "Who's there?" he demanded, his voice reaching skyward.

"Shush," I whispered, glee running away and terror taking its place. "You'll rouse the mastiff."

"Who is it?" His tone softened, yet sharpened. "Bridget?"

"Do I sound like an Irishwoman?" My wits had begun to rally, and mental functions to take hold. "What have you done with the mastiff?"

"Fed it chopped beef à la bromide." He lit another match and held it high, trying to see me—yet he did not rise to his feet. I saw that he had taken his right boot off, and his foot stuck out before him, quite swollen within its stocking, either sprained or broken.

Instantly overrun by concern, I forgot all else. "You're hurt!"

At the same time he yelped, *"Enola?"* Apparently he recognised, if not my shadowy face, then my unfortunately distinctive voice.

"Do hush. I'll get you out." Already unfastening the carpet-bag from my waist, I changed my mind and reached into my bosom first.

Sherlock demanded, "Enola, what in Heaven's name—you pop up everywhere. What—"

"One might well say the same thing of you and Mycroft, always and forever in my way. Here." I dropped a generous length of bandaging on his lap. "Wrap your foot in that. Wait." I let a little flask of brandy fall on top of the bandaging. "Drink some, for the pain. Then bandage your ankle as tightly as you can. Here are scissors—"

"No, thank you, my penknife will serve. I need nothing more, I assure you." His light had once again gone out, and I could not see his face, but I heard a tremor of laughter and, dare I say it, a kind of warmth in his voice. "Unless perhaps you have a ladder in your pocket?"

"Indeed I do." Or at least I had a rope in my carpet-bag, in order to rescue—good heavens, whom should I attempt to save first, my brother or the unfortunate Cecily? I longed to linger with Sherlock, for I felt that, given even a brief acquaintance, I could confide in him as I never could in Mycroft; I wanted to explain to Sherlock why I had run away—because I could not be corseted, either literally or figuratively, into any conventional feminine mould—and I wanted to assure him of my regard, and most especially I wanted to ask him whether he had found any communication from Mum to me when he had gone back to search her rooms at Ferndell. Never again might I have such an opportunity for conversation with my brother, unafraid that he might seize me—yet I could have wept with vexation, for there was no time! Not while Lady Cecily remained in such horrifying difficulties.

Thrusting all other thoughts aside, therefore, I demanded, "Lady Theodora hired you?"

Sherlock blurted, "How on Earth do you know of this matter?"

His unguarded reply confirmed my hope: Lady Theodora opposed the forced marriage of her daughter. "I knew it!" I cried. "I knew she would never—no such loving mother would ever—" But a fearsome thought struck me. "How was she able to approach you?"

"You seem to know all about it," Sherlock grumbled from the depths of the ha-ha, his breath seething between his teeth as he yanked at the bandaging, binding his hurt foot. "What do you think?"

"I think Sir Eustace has her confined to her chambers. So how did she manage—"

"Draw your own conclusions."

"Doing so, one must conclude that Sir Eustace has separated mother and daughter, imprisoning the latter here, judging by your presence—"

"And yours."

"Was something arranged? Is Lady Cecily expecting your visit tonight?"

Crankily he shot back, "Is she expecting yours?"

I pressed my lips together, puffing with exasperation. "Just tell me! Was something arranged?"

Silence for a moment.

Then, "No," he admitted. "I've found no way to communicate with her. Enola—"

"But you're sure she's held here."

"No secret of that. They take her out in the landau for a daily airing."

"Odd," I murmured.

"Yes, I also think it odd that they should risk her

escape for the sake of show. But perhaps a restraint of some sort, hidden beneath her clothing, binds her to the seat."

"Perhaps, but why on Earth does she not scream for help?"

Sherlock retorted, "Good heavens, Enola, the unfortunate girl is a baronet's daughter, not such a hoyden as you."

Hoyden? Was that what he called a free-thinking, independent female? As for Cecily, if he thought her meek and mannerly, he did not know her as well as I did.

"My dear brother, I will allow your insult and your ignorance to pass," I told him pleasantly. "As you are here to free Lady Cecily, evidently, I suggest we join forces, if you will promise me upon your honour not to attempt any infringement upon my liberty."

"Join—are you out of your minuscule *mind*?"

Stung, I shot back, "Am I the one in the ditch with a lamed foot?"

I fear my tone rather inflamed him. "Whatever my mischance, your place is not here. Go home, girl, where you belong."

A comment quite unworthy of him, I thought, and not deserving of a reply. Giving none, I turned my attention to opening my carpet-bag.

"For the matter of that, Enola, do you have a

home?" he continued in heightened tones. "Where are you living all this time, and how?"

Ignoring him, I extracted the rope from the carpet-bag while I mentally enumerated the latter's remaining contents: curling-irons to drive into the ground were it necessary to fasten the rope to something, a cast-iron meat tenderiser by way of club, a truncated croquet mallet, and some other tools. I hefted the bag to be sure: yes. Weight enough.

"Does any respectable and responsible older person have a care for you?"

Closing the carpet-bag, I tied one end of the rope firmly to its handle. The rest of the rope I laid out upon the ground until I was sure I had provided sufficient slack, and then I tucked a loop of its remaining length into my belt in such a manner that I would not lose it, yet could yank it free at a moment's notice.

"If not, then you cannot possibly be safe; any female dwelling alone is a magnet for crime."

Turning my back on him, I rose, and with rope trailing behind me like a tail — two tails, actually, the one to the carpet-bag and the other loose end — I strode to the nearest tree, embraced its trunk, and began to make my way upward.

I strained my every nerve and fiber in order to do so. The beech is the most difficult of all trees to climb, for the trunk is straight and exceedingly tall with smooth silver bark as glossy as satin. Only the utmost necessity—and, I admit, a great deal of petty pride; I would show the great Sherlock Holmes who needed to have a care for whom—only extremity drove me to attempt my ascent.

Gritting my teeth, wasting no breath on naughty words that came to mind, I crept upward, clinging, from time to time slipping back despite my best efforts, fervidly wishing that the blood of Darwin's monkeys ran a bit stronger in my veins as I grappled and clawed with hands rubbed raw, tried to grip with the soles of my boots—if only I could grasp with my feet, like a chimpanzee! Still, I persevered, every portion of my personage stinging with exertion, until I attained a height of perhaps twenty feet above the ground, sufficient so that I could look down on the ditch, and although I could not see into it, I felt sure that my brother, looking up, could see me—

And just as I triumphantly thought this, my head struck something.

Metal.

What in the name of the devil—

Diabolical, indeed, I discovered as I looked up to study the obstacle. Just below the point where the beech trunk began to branch, someone had placed a steel collar, the sort of thing one might use to try to keep squirrels off a bird-feeder, only much larger of course.

No wonder any villains in residence here felt safe allowing copper beeches to overhang their sunk fence. I could climb no farther.

And I fear I then whispered something quite unforgivable, for I had hoped to gain the security of the branches before I deployed the rope.

Ye gods. Ye gods in dirty breeches. Ye gods with great hopping fleas!

But I refused to admit defeat. Wasting no more breath on useless commentary, gripping hard to the beech trunk with three of my limbs, with the fourth I took the rope from my belt and began to pull up the end attached to the carpet-bag.

I required the assistance of my teeth to hold the rope each time I shifted my hand. If I should lose my grip—the consequences were barely thinkable. Meanwhile, all my limbs had begun to tremble and weaken, placing me in extreme danger. It seemed an eternity before I had it—the carpet-bag—swinging within a few feet of me. I knew I could not cling to the beech trunk much longer without falling; I needed to take aim and throw without fail, for I might have no second chance.

Eyeing a sizeable bough that jutted in the proper direction, I swung my arm so that the bag described an arc in the air, and swung once again, then once more to make sure as I let go—

The carpet-bag, as clumsy a fowl as ever flew,

blundered aloft, seemed to hang vulture-like in the air for a moment, then fell —

Yes!

Oh, yes, thank goodness. The rope lay over the bough.

Now I had only to manoeuvre until the carpet-bag wedged quite firmly in a fork of the branch. Then, at last, the rope would support me.

Meanwhile, I felt my grip upon the trunk of the tree beginning to slip.

Clinging for dear life with one arm whilst I feverishly employed the other, I pulled the rope towards me, watching the carpet-bag dangle at the other end —

Never before in my life had I truly reached the limit of my strength, and never again do I wish to repeat the experience: quite without my permission, my limbs simply let go, and helplessly I fell.

CHAPTER THE TENTH

I BADLY WANTED TO SCREAM, AND UNDER THE circumstances I certainly had every right to do so. However, any such ululation might have attracted attention of a most unwelcome sort from the house.

Somehow I retained sufficient presence of mind to utter only a squeak as I plummeted.

Also, somehow, perhaps because my extremity of terror shot new strength into me—without taking credit for any conscious virtue in the matter, I am grateful to say that somehow I kept hold of the rope.

Within a moment—a long moment, it seemed, but in fact only several horrified heartbeats—almost at once that blessed lifeline broke my fall. My carpet-bag had after all caught in the beech tree, and with a gasp I found myself swinging in midair, convulsively clutching the rope with both hands.

However, as my strength was all but gone, I slipped downward.

But even whilst swinging in such a manner, one can manipulate one's arc by leaning one's personage this way or that. Doing so, in a moment I landed with the rope still in my hands, and with the appearance of being in full control of my descent, giving barely a thump as I collapsed to the ground just where I wanted to be: near the edge of the sunk fence, but on the other side from where I had begun.

"Enola, what in the name of Heaven are you doing?" whispered my brother explosively (yes, I assure you this is possible) from the ditch.

"Is . . . it . . . not . . . obvious?" I panted, for how could he not see? I had crossed the ha-ha, and as soon as I had caught my breath, I would proceed to the house.

"It is obvious only that our mother gave birth to an Amazon." Shock vied with (I think and hope) admiration in his voice. "Why did you not tell me you had a rope? Secure it to something, quickly, then give it here so I can lift myself out of this confounded ditch."

His tone, quite accustomed to being obeyed before he could snap his fingers, failed to move me. Without, again, taking credit for any conscious virtue in the act of defiance, I responded not at all, simply because I had so thoroughly exhausted myself.

"The rope, Enola!"

"I think not," I replied blandly, my breathing somewhat more under control. "After I get back, perhaps."

"What? Back from where?"

"From locating and, if at all possible, freeing the unfortunate Lady Cecily. Would you happen to know in which room she is imprisoned?"

"In the most inaccessible apex of the north tower." He meant to discourage me, I think, and realised too late, as I sat up to dust myself off and prepare for action, that he had offered me an irresistible challenge instead. "Enola, you cannot!"

"I am not sure I can," I admitted, "but I certainly intend to try."

"It is simply not possible."

"Why? You intended to do it, before you ran afoul of the sunk fence. How did you plan to accomplish it?"

"Assist me out of this damnable ditch, and perhaps I will show you."

My tone quite gentle in contrast to his, I said, "Not until you give me your promise."

"What?"

"Promise me upon your honour that you will let me be, and will make no attempt to apprehend me or to constrain me."

Silence.

A good sign, I realised, for Sherlock Holmes would make no promise lightly. And if he gave his word, he would abide by it without fail. Indeed, if only—if we could be friends—deep within me commenced the most peculiar fluttering sensation, as if a butterfly had split open the chrysalis of my heart. Indeed, I felt my pulse begin to throb so hard that I could hear—

Hear my own heart beating?

Almost too late, I realised it was not so.

What I could hear, in that silence, was footsteps. Behind me and off to one side, someone walking. Someone had come out of the house.

And was approaching nearer by the moment.

My reaction was instantaneous and, I admit, contrary to reason: I tossed the rope to Sherlock, hissing, "Shhh! Stay down." The rope, vertical against the tree behind it, should not be noticed in the night. My brother should escape detection.

But where, pray tell, was I to hide? Instinctively I cowered, flattening myself to the ground, but what more to do—I could not think.

"...don't like it, I tell you," said a deep, dark voice I recognised; it was the massive man who had quite terrified a certain midden-picker, and who consorted most incongruously with orphans. "I haven't heard Lucifer make a sound for the past hour."

"Because the dog *isn't* barking, you roust me out of bed?" The second voice, also male, sounded childishly wrought. "Really, Father!"

"Don't pout at me, Bramwell. It's for your sake we're taking all these precautions."

Bramwell.

The Baron of Merganser's son and heir.

Then the big brute of a man was indeed, as I had concluded, the baron himself.

With fascinated horror I watched as father and son emerged from between the beech trees. Both carried heavy walking-sticks by way of weapons. The son, Bramwell, had a burly physique similar to that of his mastiff-like father, but in the younger man's case it made him resemble a toad.

As did his face, what I could see of it in the gas-lit night. Small wonder he had not managed to win a bride in any gentlemanly way.

Father and son made towards the mastiff's quarters, and at once the baron roared, "See? Someone's been feeding him!" Dramatically he pointed at the soup-bone I had flung over the fence. "Someone's poisoned him!"

"No, they haven't poisoned your darling Lucifer. Can't you hear the brute snore? He's in his bed, sleeping."

Facing the mastiff's house, they stood with their backs to me, and I took the opportunity to retreat as noiselessly as possible, scooting away hind-end-foremost, like a crustacean going under a rock, so that I could continue watching them.

"As I should be asleep in mine," added Bramwell pettishly.

"Stop being a donkey! Poison or a sleeping powder, it means the same: someone is trying to get in!"

"So?"

"Someone is prying into our affairs!"

"And what if they do? What if they pry their way right into the tower? All they will find there is a stable-boy dressed as a girl."

"Shut your mouth!" The baron's fury froze me motionless in the shadows. The way he turned on his son, I really thought for a moment that he would strike him. But instead he growled, "Not another word of that. Do you understand me? Reply."

In a subdued tone Bramwell said, "Yes, Father."

"We must arm ourselves with pistols, then search the grounds. Come along!"

"Yes, Father." Meekly Bramwell followed as the baron strode towards the house.

Even as they did so, movement from the other

direction caught my eye: swarming up the rope hand over hand as smartly as any sailor, Sherlock lifted himself from the ditch, crawling out upon the side away from me, towards the fence.

Quite sensibly, then, having concluded from Bramwell's words—as I had—that Lady Cecily was not after all to be found in the tower, he intended to make his escape. Good. Fervidly wishing to do like-wise, I stayed where I was, flat on the ground behind the nearest tree-trunk, waiting for him to depart—for I knew him to be a fox, in his way as much a danger to me as the irate baron and his unlovely son.

Sherlock rose to his feet—or, rather, his unin-jured foot, for the other, wrapped in the bandaging with which I had supplied him, showed all too clearly and unfortunately white in the night, and that pale, bloated *L* barely touched the ground; he placed hardly any weight on the foot at all. Seriously lame, he must get away as quickly as possible.

Naturally, then, I expected him to limp towards the fence. At once.

But instead, wobbling on one leg, he scanned the yard and gave a muted call: "Enola!"

Confound him! Shadowed and in hiding, I clenched my fists in frustration that he would not let me alone. Yet at the same time I felt that benighted butterfly fluttering in my heart.

"Enola, come here! I'll not leave without you."

He quite meant it, I could tell, as indeed I should have realised all along, for Sherlock Holmes was a true gentleman—that is to say, incapable of sensible behaviour under such circumstances.

Muttering the naughtiest words I knew, I rose to my feet, yanking knots out of my skirt—what a wretched time to feel shy! But I would not face my brother with my knees bared. Rife with the strangest emotions, I ran towards him while my much-rumpled brown tweed arranged itself to cover my lower limbs to the ankles.

With only the sunk fence between us I stared at Sherlock, intent on every nuance of his face. But he gave me scarcely a glance. "Enola, quick!" He tossed me the rope.

Catching it, I stood where I was, studying him for some indication, some sign . . . still he had not given me any promise, you see.

Nor would he. He only stared back at me, his chiselled face like marble, something in his gaze imploring me yet daring me to trust him, if only for this one hour of this one night.

"Confound you, Sherlock Holmes," I told him, and I took the dare. Reaching above my head to grasp the rope that hung down from the beech tree, I swung across the ha-ha to land lightly by his side.

CHAPTER THE ELEVENTH

INDEED I STOOD QUITE TOO CLOSE TO SHERLOCK for comfort, and hastily stepped back. I felt heat of embarrassment rising in my face, but surely in the dark he could not see me blushing. Continuing to move quickly, as if such had been my intention from the first, I ran to the fence and began to climb, still carrying the slack end of the rope in one hand.

Hobbling after me, Sherlock said, "Leave the blasted thing behind."

Not answering, I took the rope in my teeth instead, for halfway up the cast-iron bars I realised how my skirt was hindering me, I needed to haul it out of my way, and why should I drop the rope? It was for Sherlock; how else was he to climb with a lamed foot? As soon as I reached the fence's spiked top, I grabbed the rope, looped it around a stout paling, and tossed the end towards my brother.

Did he thank me? Heavens, no. He said, "I don't need it."

"Stop where you are!" roared the baron's voice from the direction of his Gothic manse, and almost simultaneously sounded the even louder roar of a firearm. "Stop, thieves!" The gun fired again, and I heard the bullet clang against a metal fence-post somewhere nearby.

Far from halting me, these blandishments spurred me over the fence at remarkable speed. Sherlock, too, scaled it with great alacrity, making excellent use of the rope he had said he didn't need. Indeed, by the time a third shot—or perhaps there were four? It is all frightfully rapid and muddled in my memory; my brother was letting himself down the outside of the fence, one could hear the baron and his squeaky-voiced son bellowing and running towards us, they fired once or twice more, and Sherlock fell.

"No!" I hope never again to experience such horror and desolation as I did whilst running to him, thinking that he was hit, hurt, bleeding, or worse, that he lay expiring . . .

But no! He lived. Even before I reached him, I could see him struggling to rise. Seizing his arm, I hauled him to his feet. "Lean on me," I told him; indeed, I all but carried him away, trotting. Fortunately, his weight was slight for such a tall man. "Make haste. This way." I hurried him off through a neighbouring property by a back privy-path I knew from previous explorations. "Are you badly wounded?"

"Only my pride. I slipped."

Still, such pain panted in his voice that I could scarcely believe him. "You're not shot?"

"By pistols, at that range? Hardly. They should have waited until they came closer."

He sounded quite his superior self. Relief washed through me. "Thank goodness."

"Goodness has nothing to do with it. Just listen to them."

Fearsome curses sounded not nearly far enough behind us as we ducked through a gap in someone's fence and around the corner of an unoccupied cowshed, then through the stony shadows of a neglected creamery. Leaning on my shoulder, Sherlock hobbled badly.

"Stop a moment," he whispered, panting. "Listen." He halted.

I, however, moved onward until he let go of me. Then, a few steps distant from his laboured breathing, I could hear, along with the barking voices of the baron and his son, the lilting exhortations of the Irish constable.

"For the luvva mercy, it's waking the innocent ye are," he was saying, "whilst the guilty, they're long gone."

Growl, snarl, rumble.

"To be sure, shoot all ye want on your own bit o' land, but ye can't be afther firin' pistols in the street."

More growls and snarls.

"No harm done; lookit the lovely length o' rope they lift ye. Back in t'house with ye, now. File a report in the mornin'. Yis, I'll be keepin' an eye out for thim."

In silence we listened to his tread as he returned to his beat. His measured footsteps passed nearby, then faded.

"Long gone, are we?" I muttered when all was quiet. "Would that it were so."

"You should make your escape, Enola," said my brother softly. "I will be quite all right."

Letting me go, when he had me so nearly in his clutches? One would think I might feel gratitude for his chivalry. But quite to the contrary, I became annoyed, and turned on him. "What of that loathsome baron and his beetle of a son?"

"I think we can safely assume that they have retreated." Sherlock rested his weight upon the stone slab where formerly cheese and butter had been moulded; in the darkness I could only just see him.

"They would not defy the constable, for to do so would be to draw attention to themselves."

I snorted, I am afraid, rather like a horse. "That's not what I mean at all. What have they done with the lady? It would seem that the girl you've seen coaching in the landau is a dressed-up stable-boy. The merest blind. Where is Cecily?"

During the ensuing pause I wished I could more clearly see his face. He replied slowly, "It would appear that I have been befooled, and have never actually seen the Honourable Cecily Alistair here in London."

"I have."

"What! When? Where?"

"Last week, at the—near the British Museum. Indeed, it was she whom I was endeavouring to fol-low when I was obliged to kick Mycroft."

"You *what*?"

"Our brother laid hold of me, so I booted him in the shins to get away. Did he not tell you?"

Evidently not, for Sherlock lapsed into convul-sions of laughter. Although nearly silent, he laughed so heartily that he rocked back and forth, grasping at the creamery-slab for support.

The man seemed on the verge of hysteria. It was quite time for me to get him out of harm's way. As soon as he quieted enough to be sensible—I hoped—

I told him, "Come along. We must see you home." If not straight to Dr. Watson.

Sherlock straightened, still chuckling. "I have a cab waiting at the corner of Boarshead and Oakley."

Ah. Very good. "I can lead you there by a back way."

"A shortcut?"

"Yes, by which we are less likely to encounter the constable."

"Excellent." He attempted to straighten, grimacing as his weight impinged upon his lame foot. "If you would be so good as to allow me once more to lean upon you, Enola."

I stood where I was, trying to study his face. While I had not hesitated to give him physical assistance when he was in immediate danger, I wondered now whether I could trust him. He was so clever, I would not have put it beyond him to slip handcuffs onto me before I knew what he was doing.

"Or if you would rather not," he said, correctly interpreting my stillness, "perhaps you could find me something by way of a stick or staff."

But when he said that, his voice flattened, some sort of life snuffed out, a butterfly crushed, some sentiment I would not previously have credited, but dared to detect only in its absence.

Nor did I dare to give it a name.

Yet something fluttered hard and painfully in my heart, and despite all my very sensible misgivings I walked forward to stand by his side, letting him place his hand on my shoulder.

Chapter
the
Twelfth

SHERLOCK AND I BARELY SPOKE UNTIL WE HAD passed with all the stealth we could manage through back lanes, kitchen-gardens, a carriage-drive where a sleepy watchdog barked at us, rustling hedges, creaky gates, and at last beneath someone's dark windows to Oakley Street. There we could see the cab, a substantial four-wheeler, waiting at the next corner like a chariot of Heaven beneath a halo of gas-light.

Hitching along half a step behind me, Sherlock spoke then to answer the question I had not asked. "I would be no gentleman if I did not give you my heartfelt thanks and let you go your merry way, Enola."

My heart leapt.

"But only for tonight."

So much for my leaping heart; it plummeted. My brother's caveat was just what I should have expected, yet I had hoped—never mind, but still, my disappointment stung. I responded hotly. "Why, in Heaven's name, must you continue to hound me? Can you not see—"

"I quite appreciate your remarkable abilities, my dear sister, but it is my duty to think of your future. How will you ever wed if you continue on your present course?"

No proper male could ever care for a girl who climbed trees and swung from ropes, he was saying.

"What of it?" I retorted. No one had ever cared for me; what difference if no one ever did? Still, I fear I spoke bitterly. "I am quite accustomed to being alone."

"But surely—Enola—you cannot intend to spend your life as a spinster."

This from a confirmed bachelor.

"The world is a dangerous place. A woman requires a man to protect her."

This, as he limped along, leaning more and more heavily on my shoulder. "Bosh," I told him. "If you say another word to annoy me, I will kick your sore foot."

"Enola! You wouldn't!"

"You're right," I admitted. "Rather, I would aim to lame the other one."

"Enola!" He sounded quite aghast. I think he believed me.

"No more talk of your so-called duty," I responded. "Might I remind you that it is from marriage, the so-called 'protection' of a man, that you are attempting to rescue the hapless Cecily Alistair? And might I ask how you intend to do so?"

Silence.

"Can you find out where they are keeping her?"

In a low tone he answered obliquely, "I have been a nincompoop, convinced they had her in the house. Rather than wooing the upstairs maid—"

"Ah. Bridget, no doubt."

He grimaced. "Precious little information have I got from her. What I should have done was follow the occasional carriage, even if it meant clinging to the back—"

"You cannot do that with your foot—"

"I am quite aware of the condition of my foot!" He sounded wrought. Halting, he leaned against someone's front gatepost so that he faced me. "Enola, tell me what you know of this matter, if you would be so good."

Quite pleased to spend a few more minutes in his company, but careful not to show it, I retorted, "If you will tell me what *you* know. Is Lady Theodora at liberty to contact you?"

"Unhappily so. Due to the strength of her feelings against her husband's arrangements regarding their daughter, Lady Theodora has secretly separated from Sir Eustace and, along with her remaining children, she has returned to her family's estate in the country."

Once I had learned from him the name and location of this refuge, I gladly told him all about my recent encounter with Cecily Alistair, concealing only its location, the Ladies' Lavatory. For modesty's sake, and also to safeguard my future patronage there, I called it only "a public place." But concerning the unlucky lady's grandiose escorts, her constrictive clothing, her haggard appearance, and her recognition of me, I spoke fully. I detailed her signalling with her oddly unfashionable fan, the ingenious manner in which she had slipped it to me, and the content of the invisible writing I had found upon its pink paper.

"Her chaperones were the Viscountess Inglethorpe and the Baroness Merganser," I concluded.

"You are sure of this?"

"Quite sure."

He accepted that I would not tell him how I knew. "Then they do have Lady Cecily in their clutches, and in the most desperate straits. Confound it." As if fleeing from his own thoughts, my brother lurched into a limping walk, seizing my shoulder once more for support.

I tried to offer hope. "But surely there is a limit to the infamy these people are attempting. While they can force her to the altar, surely they cannot, at the moment of truth, compel her actually to say 'I do.' "

"You credit the girl with a degree of obstinacy equal to your own, Enola."

From the quirk in his voice I could not tell whether he was laughing at me or giving me a sort of back-handed compliment.

"An attribute most unlikely," he continued, "which you of all people, having once rescued her from a Mesmerist, should know. Lady Cecily has shown herself to be susceptible to the strong will of another. She can be dominated. According to Lady Theodora, she has hardly been herself since she was abducted, and indeed shows herself to be a vessel of rather unsteady course."

"True enough," I muttered without attempting to explain how the rigours of a right-handed upbringing had forced Cecily to become two different selves, the docile public daughter versus the brilliant, rebellious reform-minded left-handed lady, who must *not* be locked into a prison masquerading as a marriage.

Sherlock continued, "Indeed, such are the accounts I have heard of her that I fear, were I to locate her and attempt a rescue, she might choose *that* occasion to scream, taking me for a kidnapper."

Nonsense. Ignoring the substance of this remark, I pounced upon its suggestion. "You have hopes of finding her, when she could be anywhere in London?"

"Hope is irrelevant. I *must* find her, or have her found, even if, as I was saying, she thinks she is being kidnapped."

"She will think nothing of the sort. Show her this." Reaching into my so-called bosom—actually a repository of numerous supplies—I brought out a pink paper fan fringed with downy pink feathers.

From my brother's throat issued a sound somewhat like the midnight call of a corn-crake, and his faltering step halted. "Is that—is that the one—"

"No. A duplicate." I handed to him this dainty item I had obtained from a caterer on Gillyglade Court. "But if she sees you with it, she will know you are her friend."

He pocketed it, saying "Thank you," but with a great deal of doubt and not much hope in his tone. "I am sure I shall look very sweet carrying it."

I rolled my eyes. "Have you a better plan?"

"Not yet."

"Nor do I." We had nearly reached the place where the cab waited; I halted. "You can manage from here, I'm sure. I'll go no farther." By shunning the illumination of the street-lamp, I hoped to prevent his seeing in full detail my costume or any other aspect of my personage. That was my only thought. I had forgotten my fears that he might attempt to seize me and take me with him in the cab.

Oddly, not until he had actually let go of my shoulder and stepped away from me did I remember once more to be afraid. He stood so much taller than I.

And so handsome, to my eyes at least, with his keen features silhouetted by an aureole of gas-light.

He said, "Will you not come along with me, Enola, have a cup of tea, and speak further of this matter?"

"Will you walk into my parlour?" said the spider to the fly. An unjust thought; Sherlock Holmes had given his word, which was inviolate; surely I could enjoy a few more hours in his company—

At the thought, my heart squeezed with a sensation so akin to rapture that I began to understand: my fear was of my own fondness for him. A few more hours in his company, and I might find myself too weak to leave. I might, like some fairy-tale denizen of the night, be caught by daylight, and captured.

I spoke almost in terror. "Some other time, thank you."

"There is no other time. The coerced marriage is scheduled to take place two days from tomorrow morning."

Ye gods!

"What!" I cried, and then a bit more lucidly, "Where?"

"That's the devil of it. I don't know."

Ye *reeking* gods!

"Bridget could tell me only that arrangements have been made to use some quite secluded chapel."

Ye gods with corns and bunions!

Sherlock said, "Are you sure you will not come with me, Enola?"

Mind and emotions all in a tumult, vehemently I shook my head. "I need to *think*," I said.

"I see. Well, in that case I can only offer you my most sincere thanks for your assistance tonight." He extended his arm, offering me his hand to shake.

Or to take hold of me. Did he think I was a fool?

Yet I would not, could not, insult his feelings by refusing. Our fingers touched, and then his gloved hand surrounded my rather grubby paw, all smirched, even bloodied, from climbing. But when I felt his grip begin to linger, I snatched my hand away.

"My dear, skittish sister," he murmured, his tone wry, almost, dare I say it, wistful, "you remind me of a wild moorland pony. Until we meet again, then, farewell." And he limped away.

CHAPTER THE THIRTEENTH

I WILL SPARE THE GENTLE READER A FULL ACCOUNT of the remainder of that night. Suffice it to say that, after watching my brother drive away in his cab, I was rent by the most unexpected and vehement sentimental eruption, a kind of Vesuvius of the emotions, that took me quite by surprise. Intermittently on my journey back to the East End I sobbed. Once I had reached my bed, I fell nearly insensible into an exhausted slumber. And in the morning when I awoke, I found myself weeping anew, unfit to be seen at breakfast. Lacking reason to dress, I remained in my nightgown; indeed, it was only a sudden, irrational terror — *What if my brother has tracked me here?* — that enabled me to leave my bed. Levitated by panic, I peered, trembling, between the window-sash and the blind. There was no sign of

Sherlock, of course, to my most exceedingly contradictory disappointment.

Indeed, all of my sensibilities seemed at odds with one another, thoughts running like frightened quail in all directions: I had failed, I could do nothing now to save the hapless Lady Cecily, nor could Sherlock with a hurt foot, I hoped it was not actually broken, I wondered whether he had gone to see Dr. Watson about it, I wondered why he had not invited his good friend Watson to accompany him into the ha-ha. I wondered where those Merganser villains were keeping their victim. I wondered where my mother might be roaming, whether she might be in any danger . . . *Don't think of Mum.* I wondered whether Sherlock had gone yet to talk with Mycroft. Confound Mycroft, he would tell Sherlock the exact location of "a public place." I must not go near the Ladies' Lavatory again, or wear a scholar's dark dress, as Mycroft had seen me in it. My alternatives in regard to disguise dwindled each time I was sighted by one of my brothers. Sherlock had seen the tweed suit; I must get rid of it. Mum had left behind a tweed suit when she had run away . . . why ever on Earth did I keep thinking of my mother? Lacking Mum, I wished Sherlock were the one who had legal guardianship of me instead of Mycroft; I sensed in Sherlock a certain sympathy . . . no. I must trust neither of them. How much had Sherlock learned of me the night before? Far too much; how could I have been such an idiot as to let him so near me for so long? Sherlock now knew that I kept numerous useful items bestowed upon my personage. Had he seen *where* I kept them? Had he noticed in the dark my womanly figure? Did he know about my bust enhancer, my dress improver, my hip regulators? Must I start all over again as Heaven knew what, perhaps a Gypsy fortune-teller, in order to elude him?

Yet—yet I so wished to encounter him again. I imagined chatting with him as we walked side by side along some cobbled London street. So many things I wished I had asked him the night before. What did he hear from Ferndell, the ancestral hall where both of us had been raised? How were Lane the butler and Mrs. Lane the cook, and their lackwit son, Dick, and the somewhat more intelligent collie dog, Reginald? What news of Kineford village? And here in London, how were Dr. and Mrs. Watson, and how was Mrs. Hudson, Sherlock's landlady, whom I had met the day I took the cipher book away? And speaking of the cipher book, *When you went to Ferndell, my dear brother Sherlock, to investigate, what did you find—what did Mum hide for me behind the mirror?*

In that moment my heart clenched, all my fluttering quail flew away, so to speak, and the volcanic tumult in my mind focussed itself with fierce, nearly insane energy upon this one question: Had Mum left any sort of message for me?

A question utterly without any practical merit.

Yet somehow, at that time of turmoil, it seemed supremely important. Because I understood, finally, why I had not yet attempted to locate Mum.

Why I hesitated to see her.

What sort of daughter I was: the frightened sort, actually.

I felt not at all sure, you see — I knew Mum cared for me in her way, but — whether she would want to see me . . .

Don't be a coward, Enola. Say it. Or if you can't say it, think it.

I did not know whether I was a fool to think Mum loved me.

But if she had left me some message in the mirror . . .

That question took over the day like so much molten lava, flooding my mind and burying any ordinary mental commerce deeper than the marketplace of Pompeii. The need I had so long postponed could be put off no longer. That morning, without some word from my mother, my life seemed not worth living.

. . .

My mother, you see, ten months ago when she had departed so unexpectedly upon my fourteenth birthday, had left behind for me a little handmade booklet of ciphers which, when solved, had led me to considerable sums of money hidden in her brass bedposts, behind her watercolours, et cetera—money that had enabled me to escape boarding school by running away in my turn. Most unfortunately, I had lost my cipher book to a cutthroat, and it had then made its way into Sherlock's hands. I had regained it by stealing it from his lodging, only to discover, by the pencil marks he had made upon the pages, that he had solved the one cipher I could not, a cipher on a page decorated with pansies:

HE SE BE RS LA IN IR
AR AS YO EN SE MY RO
TEUOEMR

Pansies look like little faces—perhaps that is why they symbolise "thoughts." Mum had affectionately called them "Johnny-jump-ups," but to me they seemed like elfin ladies with their hair piled— two dark petals on top—and on the three lighter petals below, their ancient, wizened features. If I had thought more about pansies, and less about finding something, when I saw the cipher, I might have guessed how Mum had encoded her message:

HE   SE   BE   RS   LA   IN   IR
AR   AS   YO   EN   SE   MY   RO
T   E   U   O   E   M   R

Once one has placed the three lines in order beneath one another, it is easy enough to see how Mum had arranged her letters like a pansy's five petals. And then, reading each "pansy" individually, it is simple to decipher:

HEARTS EASE BE YOURS ENOLA
SEE IN MY MIRROR

Mum had secreted something inside a hand mirror, or perhaps behind a wall mirror's brown paper backing.

Heart's ease be yours, Enola.

Mum's true wish for me? Or merest word-play? *Heartsease* is another name for pansies.

Or had Mum chosen pansies for a purpose? Might this cipher, had I solved it, have led me to the one thing I most wanted from her and the one thing I most lacked: some message of explanation, farewell, even — dare I say it — affection?

I would delay no longer; I would find out.

Instantly, the moment I resolved to act, my tears ceased along with my trembling and my barefoot pacing of my bedroom. Still in my nightgown, but all galvanised by purpose now, I seized upon my laptop writing desk, thrusting aside the papers I had left upon it previously, and sat down to communicate with Mum via the personal column of the *Pall Mall Gazette.*

I scrawled,

Mum, I never found what you left in the mirror. Please tell me, what was it?

Hmm. Quite a long message to attempt to encode.

Moreover, Sherlock and Mycroft, whom I quite wished not to know of this business, could decipher any code I knew as easily as Mum could.

Any code except this one:

My chrysanthemum: the first letter of fidelity, the third or fourth of thoughts of absent friends, the second of fascination, the second of fidelity again, the second of fascination again, the first of remembrance

In the language of flowers, you see, "fidelity" is ivy, first letter *I*. "Thoughts of absent friends" indicates zinnias, the third or fourth letter of which is *N*. "Fascination" is ferns, second letter *E*. And so on to rosemary for "remembrance." Thus far I had encoded *I NEVER*.

Egad. This would simply not do, being far too lengthy, cumbersome, and—even though I tried to use only flowers whose meanings were quite immutable—still, prone to error.

After crumpling this effort and throwing it aside, I sat frowning until I remembered how Mum had most recently communicated with me: in plain English with a veiled meaning.

After thinking about this for a while, I smiled and tried again:

Narcissus bloomed in water, for he had none.
Chrysanthemum in glass, for she had one.
All of Ivy's tendrils failed to find:
What was the Iris planted behind?

118

There! A sort of riddle, merest nonsense about flowers. Narcissus was a flower—but before the gods had turned him into one, he was the Greek youth who had fallen in love with his own beauty when he saw his reflection in a pool of water. He did not have a mirror, but Chrysanthemum, or Mum, my mother, bloomed in glass—a looking-glass. Ivy was, of course, me, and I had failed to find the Iris— another flower named from Greek mythology, Iris being the goddess who brought messages from Olympus to Earth via the bridge of the rainbow. It was a message, then, that Mum had "planted" for me, presumably behind the glass.

Much relieved, I inked copies of my riddle-rhyme for the *Pall Mall Gazette* and a few more of Mum's favourite periodicals. Since I was not yet washed, fed, or dressed, I would send these via the midday post, which would get them to Fleet Street before I could. All I needed was a few postage-stamps.

Searching for these, impatiently I cast aside the papers I had already cast aside earlier—

Until something I had written caught my eye.

A list compiled—heavens, was it only yesterday? It seemed a week ago.

Her chaperones, proud and richly clothed,
seem to be of noble blood

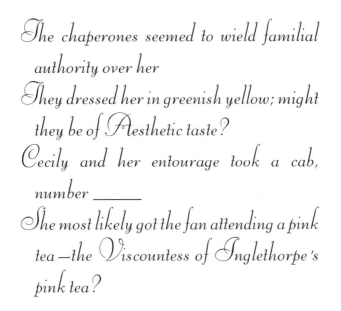

The chaperones seemed to wield familial
    authority over her
They dressed her in greenish yellow; might
    they be of Aesthetic taste?
Cecily and her entourage took a cab,
    number _____
She most likely got the fan attending a pink
    tea —the Viscountess of Inglethorpe's
    pink tea?

For a moment, reading this, I stood like a pillar
of salt in the middle of my room. Then, "Blast and
confound!" I cried, flinging up my hands in despair
of myself. "I am a dolt!" How had I let a whole morning slip away while I dithered about bygones? I
needed to get to work at once.

I knew now who might be able to tell me where
Lady Cecily was imprisoned.

CHAPTER
THE
FOURTEENTH

I NEEDED TO BE EXCEEDINGLY CAREFUL—THAT IS to say, most thoroughly disguised, for I needed to venture where I knew I should not.

Where I risked being recognised.

And what if, after all, I could not find—

No what-ifs, Enola. Just get dressed.

Easier said than done. The role I needed to take on was that of Lady, requiring a handkerchief-linen camisole and drawers to protect me from my own corset, then the corset itself (not strait-laced, of course, but necessary to support the various improvers, regulators, and enhancers that would carry my supplies whilst providing me with the requisite hour-glass figure), then a soft cover over the corset's hard corded cotton and steel, then several silk petticoats, plus the dress itself—a semi-bustled and pleated lapis blue promenade dress with jacket, suitable for shopping—and its matching hat, embroidered hand-kerchief, gloves, gaiters, and parasol. Perhaps fifteen pounds of clothing, not counting my best boots.

But that was not all.

In addition to being a Lady, today I needed to be Beautiful, as this was the guise in which I was least likely to be recognised as Enola.

So I had to take my own hair—which, like the rest of me, most unfortunately attests kinship with my brother Sherlock, being of the same dull and in-determinate tree-trunk hue as his—I had to yank my hair to the top of my head and pin it there, then hide it under my ever-so-luxuriant chestnut wig, into the coif of which I had incorporated and fastened my hat. Also I put a fringe of curls across my forehead—*de rigueur*, as Princess Alexandra wore them—and I applied various disreputable substances to my lips, cheeks, eyelids, and eyelashes as subtly as I could. After much practice, and perhaps because the blood of the Vernets runs in my veins, I am able, I think and hope, to paint my face in such a way that my art is taken for nature's own.

Then, and only then, was I ready.

Mid-afternoon, and still I had not eaten, but there was no time to do so, for my best chance—not a very good chance at all, considering that there were approximately twenty thousand cabs in London;

confound my dolichocephalic head that I could not remember the identifying number of the one cab I sought!—still, cab-drivers waited for their fares at the same cab-stands day after day, so I would begin my search at the same place and hour I had formerly seen him.

One person who might know where Lady Cecily was: the cabbie who had conveyed her shopping for her trousseau, and then, presumably, home.

I would look for him outside the Oxford Street Ladies' Lavatory.

Which was, most unfortunately, the same place where my brother Mycroft was likely to be looking for *me.*

Perambulate, I reminded myself as I descended from my own conveyance. *Mince along with itty-bitty birdy steps. Twirl your parasol. You're a beautiful lady all dressed up to go shopping.*

Off I sailed, thus, graciously, like a heavenly blue ship amid London's sooty maelstrom. Soldiers, scullery-maids, clerks and clerics, a blind beggar led by a barefoot child, a one-armed greybeard with his Victoria's Cross prominently displayed, a fuzzy-haired slum woman selling corn-plasters, gentlemen tipping their top-hats, paper-boys dotted red with skin eruptions, a ragged little girl hoarse from selling apples, an inky scholar with shoulders narrow, sloped and lopsided from carrying books—such was the grimy, motley crowd through which I strolled as if through a meadow of dark daisies.

At a genteel gait I approached the cab-stand, scanning its ranks while appearing, I hoped, only to gaze about me with idle superiority. I had no idea how I was going to find the cab I wanted, for I had not seen the driver's face, and I had no clear memory of the vehicle itself—they all looked so much the same! On the way hither I had taken pencil and paper in hand, attempting a sketch, but had produced only a blur except for the horse, which came out rather nice—I adore horses—so there I sat like a child drawing a picture of Black Beauty? Really, Enola. Disappointed in myself, I thought that perhaps when I arrived on the spot I might recognise the cab if it were there.

Too many perhaps, mights, and ifs.

I saw nothing at all familiar among the ranks of cabs.

On a nearby pavement, however, directly in my path, stood a pair of figures all too familiar to me: my brothers, Mycroft and Sherlock.

I am ashamed to say that the sight of them sent my mental faculties, along with my heartbeat, into temporary abeyance. I halted.

But then, as often happens at such moments, my

mother's voice chided from within my own mind. *Nonsense, Enola. You will do very well on your own.*

The oft-spoken, well-remembered words starched my spine. Collecting my wits, I started walking again.

Luckily, engrossed in what appeared to be a most animated conversation, Sherlock and Mycroft had not yet observed me. They stood approximately at the place where I had previously encountered — and booted — Mycroft. Dressed much as he had been that day, that robust gentleman appeared unharmed by the experience. Sherlock, however, while impeccable in his black broadcloth city suit, wore upon his right foot a carpet-slipper, and leaned heavily upon a cane.

Carefully in control of my pace and bearing, I soodled along, head up, hat fetchingly cocked, parasol aloft, making sure that I stood out like a blue beacon among the throng — *a beautiful lady who wants the whole world to give her its covert glance* — so as not to be seen. How ironic, to conceal oneself by being looked at, but there it was: my brothers had no interest in women; observing a paragon of fashionable feminine pulchritude approaching, they would give her not a second glance.

And so it proved. As I passed them, like automatons they touched their hat-brims without pausing in their conversation. ". . . cannot be allowed to go on," Mycroft was saying in his usual pompous manner. "You were much remiss, Sherlock, to let her go blithely on her errant way."

"I beg to differ. She seemed far from blithe."

Indeed? My distress had showed, apparently. Although what point Sherlock was trying to make I know not, for I heard no more, continuing on my "errant" way.

And disciplining my mind to focus on the task at hand: trying to find the cab in which Lady Cecily had disappeared.

But I still did not recognise anything familiar in the ranks before me.

Nearly at the end of the cab-stand, and out of sight of my brothers, I halted, took a deep breath, and turned to survey the scene one more time. Without any pleasing result, except that I found the humble brown gaze of a cab-horse looking back at me.

A big, placid dun horse. On impulse—for his was the most honest greeting I had received in many a day—I stepped to his head and patted his cheekbone with my silk-gloved hand. With a hay-scented snort of approval he lowered his head so that I could rub his forelock.

Sitting on his box, the cab-driver put aside his reading material—it appeared to be the *Illustrated Crime Gazetteer*—and eyed me uncertainly.

"What a sweet horse," I remarked, finding it a pleasure to speak naturally, in my own aristocratic accent. "So good-tempered. And willing, is he not?"

"That 'e is, m'lady, a 'ard worker an' a easy keeper." Warming to the topic, the cab-driver leaned towards me. "The best I ever 'ad, an' a great good fortune to a h'independent such'n as me."

He owned his horse and cab, he meant, rather than driving for a cab company, and while he kept his income, he also took his risks; a lame horse could ruin him. Smoothing the dun horse's black mane, I nodded. "He's as sturdy as a brick, isn't he? What's his name?"

"Why, 'e's a she, m'lady, an 'er name is Pet."

My smile widened. Pet snorted softly and nosed my skirt as if she might locate a treat in one of my pockets.

"Yer an uncommon good judge of 'orses, m'lady, if ye don't mind me saying so," the cabbie added. "Most of the ladies favours the fancy equipages wit 'ackneys."

"Yes, I saw one of those the other day." Eureka! Suddenly in that relaxed and idle moment I remembered! "An overlarge four-wheeler all smeared with polish," I said with unfeigned, enthusiastic disapproval, "and the horse wasn't a Hackney, but something of the sort, racy and high-headed, foaming at the bit, black with white feet all feathered like a Clydesdale's—"

"Ay, I know the one, very flashy action, knees up to 'is nose. A lot o' wasted wear an' tear if you ask me. That's Paddy Murphy an' 'is Gypsy 'orse."

"Really!" Giving Pet a final pat, I walked a few steps and climbed into the man's cab, handing him a nice shiny sum of money in advance in order to forestall hesitation or questions. "Do you think you could find this Murphy person and take me to him? I must speak with him."

"Oh, sure and begorrah, it's remimbering thim I am right enough," said the other cab-driver without hesitation, even before I had fully described a frail girl in a citrine-hued bell skirt and her two dowager chaperones. My driver had without much difficulty located Paddy Murphy in a stable-yard of the Serpentine Mews, seated upon a bale of straw with a mug of ale in hand while he offered the other cabbies a look, for a penny, at some mysterious marvel he kept in a pasteboard box. This he had put away hastily upon my arrival, standing up and tugging his cap. Now, clutching the shilling I had handed him, Paddy Murphy spoke on with true Irish loquacity. "If only because the two auld battle-axes—beg pardon, m'lady, the matron ladies—grudged me the fare, they did, and me squiring thim hither and yon all the livelong afternoon."

"Hither and yon where, exactly?"

"To be sure, if there's a linen-draper's shop in London where we dinna go, I dinna know of it. Oop one street an' down the nixt. It was looking in the shop winders they were, walking—or one uv the grand ladies walking and the other in the cab with that poor craythure uf a girrul at their beck an' call. Now and agin they'd take her inside a mercer's or some such an' I was to wait, blockin' traffic, with the coach-drivers cursing me eyes and me ancestors, begging yer ladyship's pardon, and thin we was to stop for a package, blockin' traffic some more, or wait for an order to be filled, an' the constables roarin' at me and threatenin' me license, and all the while I'm countin' on the fare . . ."

While the other cab-driver stood at my elbow as if he considered himself my escort and guardian, I listened with interest but with increasing impatience—well-concealed, I hope, for it is futile to attempt to hurry an Irishman in the telling of a tale—but I wanted to know, where did Cecily Alistair ultimately *go*?

". . . rather give it up intirely than iver go through such a riggy-ma-roll agin," Paddy Murphy was saying, "but it couldna be helped, for the poor wee

129

colleen, she could barely walk, so it seemed. And far be it from me to judge me betters, but it was none too kind to her those grand ladies was, if I do say it who shouldna be noticing."

"But I am very glad you did notice," I told him, discreetly displaying financial proof of my approval in my gloved hand: a pound note that would be his if he spoke on satisfactorily. "Please continue. Where did you take them ultimately?" I quite wanted to know where Ladies Aquilla and Otelia were hiding Cecily. "Are they staying at one of the hotels?"

"Why, no, my lady. I took them ladies an' all their packages to a place called Inglethorpe."

Viscountess Otelia's humble abode. My heart sank.

"The grandsome two, that is," added my rosy-faced informant. "But before that, the little one, the wee lassie, why, they dropped her off at a boot."

"A *what*?"

"Ay, that were the peculiarest part o' the whole peculiar business. They had me stop at a boot along the Thames, and two watermin in flat hats, they took the girrul."

A *boat*, I belatedly understood as I demanded, "Took her where?"

"Why, in the boot out onto the river, my lady. I dinna see any more."

I wanted to stamp my foot, roll my eyes, burst

out crying. Confound and blast everything! This was the last straw that broke the proverbial camel's back.

The last straw—at which a similarly proverbial drowning person might grasp. Unwilling to let even the most slender of hopes drift by.

Finding myself willing to play the latter desperate role, "Show me where," I demanded of the Irish cab-driver. "Where, exactly, you left her. Take me there."

CHAPTER THE FIFTEENTH

HALF AN HOUR LATER I STOOD AT THE FOOT OF A squalid little pier on the Thames, my nose wrinkled against stench, looking for—for Cecily Alistair? Here? It was a place even more wretched than the bleak streets where I had last found her. Down along the black water swarmed filthy beggar children, "mudlarks," scavenging bits of bone, wood, or metal from the muck. Tattooed men swaggered in and out of hulking brick buildings marked "Trawlers Ltd" or "Siam, Burma, Orient Line" or "Launches for Hire." Steamships and tall-masted sailing ships and innumerable smaller vessels crowded the straitened river whilst a hulking mechanism called a "dredger" loomed over everything, giving forth a deep roar punctuated by the curses of sailors, the shrieks of mudlarks, and the yawps of seagulls wheeling over-head. Trying to take it all in, I felt my heart sink.

Still grasping at straws, I asked the half-drunken cab-man beside me, "Did you actually *see* her being rowed away by watermen?"

"Sure and I did!"

And surely they had taken her to a houseboat or some such lodging which, unlike a hotel, could move about, changing location from day to day. Fiendishly clever. Nearly impossible to discover.

Nevertheless, I mumbled, "Which way did they go?"

He pointed upstream. I glanced in that direction, sighed, and started to turn away, utterly defeated. But something white-flecked caught my eye. Straightening, I looked again, peering at a gaggle of brown gingham in the distance.

No longer lethargic and mumbling—quite the opposite, staring like a bird dog on point—I exclaimed, "Is there an *orphanage* hereabouts?"

He answered in the affirmative, indicating a dull green mansard roof looming perhaps a block away. Instantly the noisiest possible seagull flock of memory, suspicion, and conjecture whirled into my head, all my thoughts yelling at once: little girls with shorn heads following the ha-ha man, what the deuce was his name, Baron Dagobert Merganser, in his sister-in-law's mansion; why not his own home? Perhaps because he did not want it known who he really was? But why had he been consorting with orphans at all? He seemed hardly the charitable type. And why at such a ticklish time, when he was holding his well-to-do niece captive to force her to marry his son—

. . . arrangements have been made to use some quite secluded chapel.

Oh. Oh, my goodness. *Did orphanages have chapels?*

It seemed probable that they did, but I did not know for sure, and I should have investigated the matter thoroughly, of course, for it might have been the merest coincidence that there was an orphanage near this particular pier on the Thames; moreover, the orphans I had seen at Inglethorpe might have come from a different institution altogether, their presence might have signified nothing, et cetera—

Yet, as my brother Sherlock would have said, it was suggestive, was it not? A chance offered itself, and there was no time for research and hesitation: the unfortunate Lady Cecily was to be forcibly wed *tomorrow morning.*

Desperate measures were called for.

Two hours later, walking towards the Witherspoon Home for Waifs and Strays, I tried to see something to indicate the presence of a chapel—a stained-glass window, for instance — but I observed only the upper part of an exceedingly plain three-storey stone-and-plaster edifice surrounded by a tall wooden fence with its vertical planks so close-set, one could not even peep through the cracks. Most unattractive, that barrier, and most uncompromising.

I found it easy enough, at that point, to look as if I were about to weep.

This being exactly the effect I desired. I was got up as a waif. A rather tall waif, but a waif nevertheless. In order to present a stick-thin, indeed cadaverous figure, I had put aside all my improvers, regulators, and enhancers — no small decision, as along with them I put aside my defensive armour — corset and dagger — and most of my usual supplies. I carried with me only a few carefully selected items in my pockets.

These did not include food, and there had been no time to eat; my stomach yowled with hunger, and I felt a bit faint — well, so much the better for the impression I needed to make. With a combination of vinegar and soap I had rendered my skin pasty and blistered, and a touch of lamp-black made my eyes appear haggard, my cheeks hollow. My own hair, allowed to tangle down my back, was quite ugly enough for any ragamuffin, especially after I had rubbed it and myself with coal-ash. I wore the midden-picker's exceedingly humble and dirty clothing, hanging far too large upon my bony shoulders and chest, and I had even gone so far as to tear some rips in the cloth. My feet I wrapped with rags. On my head, indeed almost covering my eyes, I had placed a bowler hat rescued from the street, well squashed by horses' feet and carriage wheels. As a pauper girl will use any such item to keep her head warm and covered, the effect was, I thought, most salubrious.

As was my hesitation. Anyone watching would see a waif trying to gather courage to venture into the fenced and forbidding unknown, not quite decided to give up her starveling freedom for the sake of food, a shorn head, and domestic servitude. They could not possibly know that the vacillating waif was actually an aspiring Perditorian not quite decided whether she really needed to risk contacting her brother.

Indeed, after pacing the area of the orphanage awhile, making sure there was only one way to get in or out, I retreated.

But only for a brief period of time, during which I pencilled a note, expressing much greater certainty than I actually felt, as follows:

Sherlock,
  Shortly prior to nuptial travesty,
E.H. will attempt to exit Witherspoon

orphanage, 472 Huxtable Lane, with pink fan. Meet her at gate; I leave it to you to assist her from there.

E.H.

With greatest trepidation I folded this and addressed it to 221b Baker Street, for all my instincts warned me against giving my brother the slightest idea where I might be found at any particular time. Certainly he would try to trace the message back to me — no matter, for I would not remain in the same place, and any description a messenger might give of me would tell him only that I had disguised myself as a beggar — but what if, on the morrow, he engaged assistance, not only to rescue Lady Cecily, but to ensnare me?

Yet I had no choice. For the sake of the hapless lady I must risk myself in more ways than one.

I gave the message to a licensed commissionaire; very surprised and puzzled he was to accept such a literate communication and substantial fee from a wretch such as I appeared to be, but I knew he would deliver the note without fail; that was his duty.

Then, as there was no time to hesitate any longer, I walked — or staggered, rather, for beneath my ragged and filthy skirt I kept my knees bent, in order to shorten my height whilst simulating a crippling case of rickets — I made my way back to the Witherspoon Home, applied to my eyes a rag in which I clutched a bit of onion in order to produce some tears, then knocked on the gate.

"Name?" asked an exceedingly plain matron seated at a rather inadequate desk, filling out a form for me.

"Peggy, mum." Standing before her, I had to remember to keep my knees bent. The effort caused me to sway a bit. So much the better.

"Surname?"

"Just Peggy, mum."

"Parents?"

"Not what I ever 'eard of, mum." In the broadest Cockney accent I could manage, with a sniffle. Too tall to seem quite pathetic otherwise, I had decided to be lachrymose and simple.

With a sigh the woman marked a box: *Illegitimate*. But she tried once more. "Date and place of birth?"

"I don't rightly know, mum."

"Baptism?"

"What's that, mum?"

"Have you been baptised?"

" 'Ow wud I know, mum?" Tears in my tone, and my stomach also audibly lamented.

The matron looked at me, then lifted a little Chinese bell from her desk and tinkled it. The shape of the bell, sans handle, was the same as the shape of her monumental white cotton cap.

At the summons of the bell, a little girl came in who looked exactly the same as all the other little girls in the place: unsmiling stare, cropped hair, brown gingham pinafore over an even uglier brown frock. "Yes, Matron?"

"Bring bread and tea, child."

"Yes, Matron." The girl bobbed and departed.

"Sit down, Peggy," said the matron kindly to me. "Have you ever been incarcerated?"

"What's that, mum?"

"Have you ever been put in prison for any crime?"

"No, mum."

"Have you ever been in the workhouse?"

And so it went. While I sat, shaking with nerves and hunger, shedding occasional tears, and gobbling (quite sincerely) a great deal of plain bread and weak tea, she determined that I had little if any education, had not attended Sunday school, did not possess any money or any friends or relatives to pay for my care, had not received parish relief, and had not been treated for scrofula, scarlet fever, whooping cough, or smallpox.

"Subject to fits?"

"No, mum."

"Incontinence of urine?"

"Beg pardon, mum?"

She puffed her thin lips, then with visible effort made herself say, "Do you wet yourself or your bed?"

"No, mum!"

"Very well, ah"—she cast her eye back over the papers she had just filled out—"Peggy." Laying down her pen, she rang her bell again, and this time a girl about my age came in carrying an armload of clothing in which brown gingham predominated. "You have had enough to eat for the time being. Go along with this little woman now, have a bath, and then I will check you for, ah, any infections or infestations, and cut your hair."

The moment for which I had been waiting.

"Cut my hair, mum?" Wide-eyed, I wobbled to my feet. "But mum, I don't want my hair cut."

"You must have it cut if you are to stay here, child."

"But, mum—"

"Do you wish to be fed, clothed, and educated? If so, you must have your hair cut in a hygienic manner. And you must be vaccinated against smallpox."

"You—mean—a *needle*, mum?" This was an unexpected chance for me to pretend even greater terror—every Cockney has a horror of vaccination—and I took full advantage of it. "I can't stand no one puttin' no pision in me wit no needle, mum!"

"Nonsense. It's not poison, and of course you can stand the prick of a needle; every girl here has done so."

The starch and scorn in her tone were just what I needed to help me truly cry out loud. "I don't know if I can bear it, mum!"

"Well, then you must go back out on the street."

"No, mum, please, I'm 'ungry."

"Then if you wish to stay, you must do as I say. Decide."

As if in a frenzy of despair and vacillation I raised my clasped hands. "I can't decide! I needs to pray on it. A few minutes to pray on it, mum. Is there a chapel, mum?"

She eyed me suspiciously, but my unexpectedly devout request could hardly be refused, especially not in front of the "little woman" standing there — sullen, silent, and probably required to pray several times a day.

"Very well," she muttered, looking up to instruct the girl. "Take her to the chapel — "

Eureka!

" — then return to your regular duties. I will check on her in a few minutes."

A few minutes were all I needed.

Once the indifferent waif-in-waiting had showed me to the chapel—a dim little sanctuary constructed as an ell of the main building—the instant its holy doors had closed behind her retreating personage, I sprang from my pew, whisked up the pile of clothing the girl had deposited beside me, and took cover. I was hiding under the pulpit when I heard the matron come in.

"Child?" she called. *"Child?"* And after a pause, during which most likely she consulted her papers regarding my name, "Peggy, come here at once!"

I did not, of course.

Grumbling aloud, "Where can the nitwit have got to?" she went out again, to inquire, and as soon as she had done so, I set myself to find a better hiding place in case I were truly searched for. It has been my observation that people playing hide-and-seek peer into things and under things, downward but hardly ever upward. Also, climbing is my forte. For both of those reasons, upward I went, with no trouble at all ascending the tall, ornately carved cabinet of the pipe-organ and slipping first my new clothing—which I had done up into a bundle for easy carrying—then my personage onto its sturdy canvas top. There, cradled by that dust cover, inches from the chapel ceiling, surrounded by the organ cabinet's aspiring cornice, I lay in relative safety and complete comfort when the matron came back, with a few companions, for another look.

I heard them, rather than saw them, poking about:

"I imagine she's got cold feet and gone."

"Towheedle at the gate says not."

"He's been napping again, then, for how else can she have got out? And she's not here."

"She might be wandering the halls. She's none too bright."

"She'll go where she smells food, mark my words."

"We must keep guard on the kitchen, then."

"Well, she's certainly not in this chapel." They stood almost directly under me. "We must tell everyone to be on the lookout —"

"What a nuisance," one of them complained, "and tonight of all nights, when we have so much preparation for tomorrow."

My interest quite heightened, I assure you.

"A wedding, of all things, here?"

It has to be Cecily, it has to be, I have got it right, yes!

As inwardly I rejoiced, the speaker went on, "What an odd —"

"One must not ask questions," someone shushed her. "The baron has promised a great deal, not just funds but favours of all sorts."

Including, I supposed, "treats" such as the visit to "his" house.

"The attic room's not yet ready," continued the complainer, "and there's all the flowers to be got in."

"Come along, then, we're wasting time."

I heard them leaving.

"The girl will turn up."

"God forgive me, I quite hope she doesn't." I recognised the voice of the matron who had evaluated me saying, as they went out the door, "She's a terribly repulsive ragamuffin, not at all the sort of thing one would wish the baron to encounter here."

Oh ho, I thought, my nerves steadied by a moment of amusement. Little does she know.

CHAPTER
THE
SIXTEENTH

IN MY NEST ATOP THE PIPE-ORGAN I ACTUALLY napped, with my belly full of bread and nothing to do but stay where I was until waifs, strays (what was the difference between a waif and a stray, I wondered), and bell-headed matrons had retired for the night.

Evening prayers awoke me—indeed, nearly deafened me even though I plugged my ears with my fingers; my entire personage vibrated. The experience shook me in more ways than one, for I heard the organist remark on her way out that there was something odd and muffled about the tone of the instrument. I lay quite still for an hour or more afterward, but as nothing came of it, my ears stopped ringing, and all seemed quiet, finally and cautiously I climbed down—feeling my way in utter darkness.

First, however, I stripped off my rags, leaving them atop the organ. Underneath them, having planned as thoroughly as possible, I wore a simple muslin frock. The bundle of orphanage clothes I carried with me as I shuffled and groped towards the altar in order to light some candles.

I must admit that, even though I am a free-thinker and a rationalist, I felt quite queer helping myself to the holy tapers in this fashion. And, after I had provided light, I felt even more discomfited as I washed myself with the water in the baptismal font. There is something intimidating about a shadowy chapel at night, and once I had tidied my hair into a simple bun and removed every possible vestige of "waif" from my appearance, I felt quite eager to go elsewhere.

Specifically, I wanted to find the attic room that was being got ready for the baron.

I reasoned that Lady Cecily Alistair would be brought to this orphanage quietly, by boat, perhaps before dawn, for the unfortunate girl was to be married to the toad-like Bramwell Merganser under duress, and therefore in secrecy. Usually, a bride-to-be of the upper classes would be coached to the church in her wedding-gown; perhaps they might dress up the stable-boy—but no, any show of wedding finery would surely excite comment and inquiry. Baron and Baroness Merganser needed to complete their unsavoury deed and have it a fait accompli before any boasting could ensue.

Yet I could not conceive of such a proud pair forgoing all of the usual marital pomp. *You will need a trousseau, and a trousseau you shall have* . . . poor Cecily. Surely Aquilla and Otelia would force her to dress the part of a blushing bride.

> **Premise: They will require her to wear a wedding-gown.**
> **Premise: Circumspection requires that they will not bring her to the orphanage actually wearing the gown.**
> **Conclusion: They will put the gown on her in situ.**

Hence the attic room; for what other purpose could it be needed? Presumably all other chambers in the place were occupied by waifs—or strays—whichever—and a bride requires a certain privacy.

Especially when it is not her idea to be a bride.

Tomorrow morning, when Cecily Alistair was brought in to be all dressed in white, I quite wanted to be there, hidden and waiting.

Slipping out of the chapel door, I found hallways dimly lit by gas turned to its lowest flame, and in the near distance I heard the creaking tread of a matron, then her murmur as she accosted a wayward child: "What are you doing out of bed?"

Oh, dear. It seemed that an orphanage never truly slept. How fortunate that, outwitting brother Mycroft last summer, I had become quite adept at walking silently upon stocking feet. As quickly and silently as I could, I crept away from the matron, located a stairway, ascended it to the first storey, then the second, then, eureka! In darkness I climbed a final narrow stairway to what must be the attic door.

Locked, of course.

But only with a simple, old-fashioned latch, the sort I knew how to pick. I did so, opened the door, stepped inside, closed the door silently behind me, then with a sense of triumph I lit a candle I had brought with me from the chapel. Raising it, I saw —

Steamer-trunks, an empty birdcage, broken rocking-horses, and the like, with dust enshrouding everything.

For a horrible, sinking moment I could not understand what dreadful mistake I had made. This was not the first time my reasoning had been wrong, wrong, wrong. I was after all only a stupid girl, unfit to —

Nonsense, Enola. Think.

I thought, and realised that such a large building would have more than one attic. I must try again, that was all.

And so I did, and eventually succeeded. I will spare the gentle reader any account of the ensuing several hours and near-encounters except to say that finally, just at dawn and with huge relief, I found myself in what was obviously the right place: an attic room cleared, cleaned, scrubbed, shined. With a dressing-table, a standing mirror, and some chairs.

And with quite an imposing ghostly white presence hanging from a rafter to puddle on the floor.

White on white. Draped in a sheet to keep it clean, this looming spectre was the wedding-gown, a titanic one, its crystal-beaded lace train trailing a good nine feet.

Close by hung a similarly beaded, elaborate head-piece with yards of cloudy white veil.

And near at hand stood the most peculiar pair of white shoes—slippers, rather, their fine leather uppers daintily shaped, but with soles like the clogs gentlewomen sometimes wore to elevate themselves above the muck of the street. Yet even taller. Soles that would put the wearer at least ten inches above the ground. Wearing those shoes would be like trying to walk on stilts.

It took me a moment to comprehend: how wickedly clever! A way to hobble the bride without letting it show, and at the same time to make her look older, taller, and more splendid in the expensive gown.

Poor little Lady Cecily, who wanted only to read, draw, think, and do some good in the world, to spend her life at the dubious mercy of Viscountess Otelia and Baroness Aquilla?

"Harpies," I muttered. "Vipers. They must be defeated." My unlucky lady must be saved.

But first I must find a place to hide until it was time.

And this necessity, which I had considered would be the least of my worries, turned out to be most troublesome. I blew out my candle and, after it was cool, secreted it in my pocket; would that my long and lanky personage could so easily be concealed! By the dawn light streaming in through dormer windows I looked high and low, but there was simply no cover to be found in that bare attic. No sofa behind which to crawl, no wardrobe or other bulky furniture, no concealing draperies, not even a cloth skirt upon the table.

And as I stood there, in plain sight, I heard footsteps ascending the attic stairs.

Ye gods! Now what?

Only one possibility presented itself, which I acknowledged with the greatest reluctance, for it caused in me a revulsion of feeling even worse than that which had afflicted me whilst appropriating altar candles and baptismal water. Why so I cannot say, for I love beautiful clothing, and the gown was exquisite—princess seaming, puffed sleeves, gleaming silk overlaid with dainty lace, as I saw when I forced myself to lift the sheet and look. Yet the sight of all that white appalled me. I hesitated until I heard someone actually at the door before I took a deep breath, steeled myself as if entering the sea from a bathing machine, and dived under the heavily beaded hem to stand up within the hanging gown. Dangling my bundle within the fullness of its gored skirt, I placed my feet so that its train would hide them. As I then stood quite still, it settled around me naturally enough.

Or so I hoped.

I heard multiple footsteps; several persons were entering the room. I heard a leaden sort of thump or thud, and then a matriarchal voice said icily, "Very well, Jenkins, I think she is unlikely to cause any mischief here. You may remove the restraint from her mouth."

The—the harridans, the hags, the—no appellation seemed forceful enough—the viragoes had *gagged* her? Wanting a look at Lady Cecily, some indication of how she was bearing up, I peeped through a placket near the wedding-gown's waist, but without much success. In a fragmentary manner I saw:

A lopsided derriere much draped in mauve and cream. That would be Viscountess Otelia.

Just as elaborately clad in dove-grey silk not an inch of which went unadorned, another figure quite similar to the first: the charming Aquilla.

A simple flowered skirt with the tails of white lace apron-ties hanging down: a chambermaid in her morning dress.

All three of them turned towards a fourth person who had apparently flung herself into a chair on the other side of the room, as far as possible from the gown in which I hid. Of this individual I could see only a bit of citrine: the same awful bell skirt they had put on Cecily when I had first seen her in the Ladies' Lavatory.

I felt a pang both of pity and of triumph: my little left-handed lady had more spirit than Sherlock Holmes would have credited. Obviously she had not ceased resisting.

It was Aquilla (ruched, ruffled, pleated, poufed, flounced, fringed, beaded, beribboned, bedecked beyond description) who had spoken, and now continued, "Do the best you can with her, Jenkins. We must see to the altar flowers. *You*," to the lump of citrine rebellion in the chair, "put a better face on, or there will be hobbles for you as well as the shoes, and no dinner afterward; you will watch the rest of us enjoy your wedding feast. Come, Otelia. We will return shortly." She said this over her shoulder to Jenkins as the two of them rustled silkily out the door.

As soon as they moved, I could at last see Cecily fully. With her head down she slumped in her chair like a comma, despair written in every line of her personage. Although she looked not much thinner than when I had last seen her—they could not, after all, starve her entirely, lest she die—still she seemed in some less tangible way diminished. Her face more frail and elfin, her eyes more shadowed. Seeing her thus, I bit my lip in consternation, for what if she no longer had the necessary strength?

"Now, Miss Cecily," coaxed the maid, Jenkins, "sometimes a body's got to just make the best of what'll be better when it's over. Now, just think how pretty you're going to look, all done up in orange blossoms and myrtle, with the sweetest wee gros-grain ribbons—did you see the dear, dear ribbons Lady Aquilla got for your bouquet?" Crossing the room, the maid picked up a large bandbox someone had left on the floor inside the door, placed it on a chair, lifted its lid, and bent over it to search its contents.

Her attention fully diverted.

My chance.

From one of my pockets I drew a certain peculiar pink fan. Then, from inside the wedding-gown I opened the placket and poked my head out, holding the fan to my chin as a signal, so that Lady Cecily would be sure to recognise me and understand what I was about.

If only she looked up!

She did. My movements caused her to lift her head and stare at me. I felt once again that sense of electric shock when our gazes met and locked — shock especially keen, I am sure, on her part, under the circumstances; her great, dark eyes widened enormously.

Pointing to the oblivious servant, I silently mouthed the words, "Send her away."

How Cecily was to do this when the servant was under strict orders to stay with her, I had no idea. But as it turned out, she accomplished the task with marvellous efficiency even as I drew my head back into the snowy concealment of the gown; she simply slid from her chair with a thump to sprawl on the floor in what appeared to be a faint.

"Miss Cecily?" I heard the maid inquire, and then, punctuated by sounds of movement, a series of panicky cries. "Miss Cecily! Miss Cecily, wake up! Oh, my goodness! Smelling-salts! A doctor! Help!"

The good Jenkins fled the room.

The instant I heard her exit, I darted out—rather like a partridge breaking cover—I burst from under the wedding-gown and across the room to close the door and turn the key in the lock even as the maid's frantic feet thumped down the attic stairs.

"There!" I whispered, feeling quite a triumphant grin on my face as I turned to Cecily.

She still lay motionless on the floor.

Heavens, it wasn't just a clever ploy. She had truly fainted.

What if I could not revive her?

CHAPTER
THE
SEVENTEENTH

BUT AS I KNELT BESIDE HER, CECILY GAVE A LITTLE sigh, blinked, opened her eyes, and as her gaze fixed on my face, joyous amazement dawned. With greatest wonder she whispered, "Enola?"

How strangely it affected me to hear her say my true name in that way. Gripped by emotion, I could neither move nor speak.

"Enola?" Her hands faltered towards me. "You, again, can it be?"

"Shhh." Her touch made me want to weep, but I quite needed to function. Forcing myself into action, I fumbled in my pockets for the strengthening candies I always carried with me, unwrapping one and giving it to her. She placed it in her mouth and, galvanised, I think, more by my presence than by sugar, sat up—to find me pulling off her shoes. "We are going to disguise you," I told her softly but with clear emphasis, "so that you can escape. Agreed?"

"Agreed? By all means, my mysterious friend!" Springing to her feet, Cecily began to claw at her diabolical skirt to get it off. The confounded thing fastened in back, of course, as did her blouse; one of the requisites of upper-class clothing is that one should not be able to dress oneself without the assistance of a servant. After I had torn open her buttons, she sloughed off her outer garments, letting them puddle on the floor as I ran for the bundle I had left beneath the bridal-gown.

The bundle of garments, including a coarse leather pair of boots, that had been offered to "Peggy" the afternoon before. "We are going to make an orphan of you."

"Indeed, I might as well be one!" Still, Cecily's thin face lit up when she saw the things—she did not look nearly so much like Alice in Wonderland when she was glad—and she snatched at them.

As I, also, was in a tremendous hurry to undo the bundle and get the garments onto her, it became exceedingly difficult to accomplish simple tasks; Cecily and I kept getting in each other's way. Moreover, I had things to tell her. "You remember Mr. Sherlock Holmes?"

Joyously she responded, "Your brother!"

"Heavens!" She took my breath away. "I hope you have not told anyone?"

"Of course not. Did you tell anyone about my charcoal drawings?"

The question was rhetorical; she knew I had not. Trying to hide my smile, I hurried on. "Your mother has retained Mr. Holmes on your behalf. She has gone to stay with her family in the country. He will take you to her. Confound these stockings!"

It seemed to be taking an eternity for us to dress her in the brown smock and brown gingham pinafore, thick zebra-striped stockings, and sensible (ugly) boots. But in actuality it must have been only a very few minutes, for no one had yet returned as I tried to tuck her hair under her white ruffled cap.

Long, glossy, thick, slithery hair, it kept getting away from me.

"This will not do," I whispered, growing a bit wrought, aware of moments ticking away. "How are you going to pass as an orphan with such accursedly lovely hair?"

"Just cut it off!"

"We haven't the time!" Yet I grabbed scissors out of the bandbox—small things meant for snipping ribbon, they would have to do—and started hacking off her shining locks at the level of her ears.

No sooner had I begun than we both heard footsteps pounding towards us up the attic stairs. Cecily startled like a deer.

"Hold still!"

Rigid, she did so, but started to say, "Enola, thank you for—"

"Shhh. Make no sound," I whispered, frantically cutting off long tresses of hair and stowing them in my pockets for lack of any other place to hide them.

Someone, probably Jenkins, tried the door-knob, then cried, "It's locked!"

Yet, as is the case with most people, she continued to agitate the knob as if somehow she could thus release the bolt.

"Get out of my way," commanded either the baroness or the viscountess—they both sounded the same. "You nitwit, she tricked you." A series of thumps ensued as if someone had actually pushed the unfortunate Jenkins down the stairs! At the same time the fierce voice exhorted, "Cecily!"

That shout made the girl flinch; I felt her jump. "Shhh," I whispered, still snipping my way from one ear around the back of her neck to the other. "Pull your front hair down over your face."

As she did so, the knob rattled anew. "Cecily, open this door and let us in," shrieked one of the sisters.

"Open up at once!" screeched the other.

They continued thus in counterpoint. "Cecily! Ungrateful brat!"

"Open this door or I will punish you severely!"

Et cetera.

After a brief time, however, the tenor of their tune changed. "There must be another key," one of them declared. "Jenkins, go find it!"

Oh, dear.

But I was nearly ready. "There," I whispered, scissoring a thick swath across Cecily's forehead. "Finished." Once more I popped the cap on her head, and a dear little orphan she made indeed, standing a foot shorter than I, in overlarge shoes and clothing too big for her, as if she were expected to grow into it. Her shorn hair, especially the thatch hiding her forehead, made her nearly unrecognisable as Cecily Alistair. "Splendid!"

She could not answer my smile; her huge eyes remained terrified as they fixed on me for salvation. "But, Enola, now what? How —"

How, indeed, to effect her escape with the enemy's voices clamouring directly outside the attic?

"Bring men to knock the door down!" shrilled an aunt.

"And be quick!" screeched the other.

"Yes, my lady. Yes, my lady." Jenkins's voice faded below.

Cecily bit her lip as if to keep from sobbing.

"Trust me," I told her, scooting over to where the wedding-gown hung. Ripping off its sheet as I snatched it down off its hanger, I plopped it onto myself.

I would not have thought it possible for Cecily's eyes to stretch any farther. But widen yet more they did, and her rosebud mouth formed an O.

"To give you time," I whispered. "Here." Burrowing under the gown to the pocket of my muslin dress, I found the pink paper fan, on which I had pencilled as a contingency, lest all else fail:

I instructed Lady Cecily, "Hide behind the door. When they have all come in, slip out. Go to the gate, show this"—I handed her the fan—"and Mr. Holmes, or one of his friends, should be waiting for you."

Meanwhile, footsteps pounded up the attic stairs again. "Here's an extra key, my lady," cried a shaky voice outside.

There was no time to fasten the myriad pearl buttons running up the wedding gown's back. I had just a moment to seize the headdress and plop it into place on myself, covering my face with layers of cloudy veil, as I threw myself into the chair in which Cecily had been sitting.

The key snicked in the lock.

So long as I slouched in the chair, mostly buried in mounds of wedding-gown, they would not see how tall I was, their suspicions would not be aroused—so I hoped, as I hid my stocking feet under yards of white skirt and my hands in my lap, pinning folds of veil between my fingers.

"Cecily!" stormed two harridan voices in unison as the door slammed open. Then, similarly in chorus but quite changed in tone, *"Cecily?"*

Through my milky thickness of veil I could not make out their expressions, the two dowagers and the cowed servant, as they walked in and formed a semi-circle, staring at me.

"She's put her gown on," one of them said in wondering tones.

I could only dimly see them—and behind them, a little orphan girl tiptoeing out of the room to slip down the stairs. In order to keep attention firmly upon myself whilst Cecily made her escape, I began to rock my upper body to and fro in an interestingly demented manner.

"Cecily, stop it."

"Why have you put your dress on by yourself? You've got it all crooked. Stand up."

Instead, I feigned a sort of spasm.

"Stop that grotesque twitching, Cecily! What's the matter with you? Let me see you." One of them tried to lift my veil.

She could not, of course, as I was holding it down. I tried to assess how far the real Cecily might have got by now. Downstairs, surely, and possibly out the door, crossing the yard?

"Cecily! Let go of that veil!" One of the sisters tried to wrest it from me.

"Don't, Otelia, you'll tear it, and that's the finest tulle in London!"

"You make her let go, then!"

"Cecily!" Aquilla grasped me bruisingly by both upper arms. "Do as she says."

Instead, I began to thrash in a truly pitiful manner.

"Cecily!" Both of them grasped me by the shoulders, shaking me, to my satisfaction; let them maul me all they liked. The only difficulty was to remain stubbornly silent while they abused me, so as not to let my voice give me away. The longer they belaboured me, the better, giving the real Cecily time to escape.

But they were interrupted. "What's the matter

with her?" roared a male voice—unmistakably that of the baron.

Both baroness and viscountess squeaked in well-bred shock at such a masculine invasion, turning on him. "Dagobert! Bramwell!" squawked, presumably, Aquilla. "What are you doing here?"

Heaven help me, both of them? Yes, through my veil I could make out two looming forms in fancy dress.

"Jenkins said we needed to break down the door," replied the baron. "Is Cecily misbehaving?"

"I think she's gone quite mad!"

It was quite simple for me, in my terror of the baron, to act the part of a lunatic, recommencing to rock to and fro in my chair, but this time allowing myself a number of pathetic moans.

The baroness continued, "First she fainted, or pretended to, and then she locked us out, and now she's gone and rucked her gown all over herself; just look at her! Nod, nod, nodding like a—"

Abruptly the Baroness of Merganser stopped, and when she spoke on, it was in the tone of one who has taken command in a crisis. "Jenkins, fetch the vicar up here."

"Yes, my lady." I heard the hapless servant scamper away.

"Bramwell, come stand beside your bride."

"What are you talking about, Mother?" whined that toad-like individual.

"Do as I say! Don't you see the state she's in? And she'll only get worse; do you think we want to carry her down to the chapel? No, ceremony can go hang; we must get you married to her here and now."

CHAPTER
THE
EIGHTEENTH

"JOLLY GOOD IDEA! HA-HA!" ROARED THE BARON.

And in that awful moment I understood my instinctive reluctance to secret myself within bridal white. It had to do with the *lock* part of the word *wedlock*. Trapped. Horribly, irrevocably trapped—

Nonsense, Enola. You will do quite well on your own. Think.

Although terribly frightened by the unexpected turn of events, I reasoned that I was no worse off than before. At one point or another I must take very hasty leave, that was all. And as we all waited for the vicar to arrive, even as I squirmed and swayed, whimpered and groaned, doing my best to seem demented, perversely my thoughts and sentiments calmed so much that, despite my awkward situation, I found myself pleasantly contemplating the possibility of a most unforgettable scene. Like my brother Sherlock, I dearly love a moment of drama now and then. I would play my lunatic part, I decided, until the very moment when they would try to make me say, "I do." At which point I would quite lucidly declare, "I most definitely do *not*," and then—as they all stood in shock and astonishment that I should so forcefully reject the charming Bramwell—then with great dignity and decision I would arise from my chair, rip off my disguise, and stalk out.

Or, more realistically, run like the devil.

Without any shoes?

Oh, well. One must be brave; do or die; certainly Cecily had gotten away by now, making my predicament worthwhile—such were my musings as I rocked, twitched, grunted, and occasionally panted for better effect. The wedding-gown had the currently fashionable, bead-encrusted steel-stiff high collar, and this "dog collar"—all too appropriate for these so-called nuptials—rasped against my earlobes most annoyingly, causing me to hiss with pain as well as swaying, shuddering, et cetera. I have that tormenting collar partly to thank for the convincing quality of my performance.

"Most irregular," the vicar was murmuring as Jenkins brought him in.

"You see how she is?" Aquilla demanded.

"Well, yes, I do appreciate—"

"Appreciate also **how well** you will be rewarded, ha-ha! And get on **with it!**" bellowed an unmistakable voice.

Someone, probably Jenkins, thrust a fragrant bouquet into my lap and stuck some flowers onto my bobbing head whilst the others milled around, pushing aside the few chairs, taking their places and asking one another who had the rings. As if herding cattle, Aquilla lashed—with her tongue—and in a surprisingly brief time the vicar did, indeed, get on with it.

"Dearly beloved," he intoned, "we are gathered here today to join this man and this woman in holy matrimony . . ."

Holy, my eye. While continuing to bob, spasm, and so on, I paid close attention to the vicar's drone, waiting for my cue.

"If anyone here present doth know any just reason why this man should not be joined with this woman in marriage, let him speak now—"

All quite routine. No one ever said anything.

"—or forever hold his peace."

"I can think of several reasons," spake a pompous male voice from the doorway.

My resultant squeak went unnoticed in the generalised gasp of shock as all turned to the intruder. The baron demanded, "Who are you?"

But I already knew who it was. The worst of all

possible uninvited guests, he whom I feared above all others, the person in all the world who had the most power to ruin my life—

The way he had just ruined my surprise.

Truly it is amazing what disappointed vanity will do: instantaneously, supreme spleen replaced my feelings of terror. Outraged, "Mycroft," I shouted as I shot to my feet and snatched the veil off my head, "curse you, why can't you let me—"

"First, although not foremost, that the bride is not who she is purported to be." Mycroft spoke on in the same pontificating tone, unblinking, whilst screams and exclamations burst from all others.

"—let me *alone*!" In a frenzy of wrath I ran at him and, with both hands upraised as if hurling a boulder, I threw my bridal veil onto his head.

Alas that I could not pause to admire the effect as I crowned him from top-hat to waistcoat in white lace and tulle. I am sure his appearance was most startling. But in the act I had regained just enough sense to run on past him. As my arms came down, so did the bridal-gown, falling off me to puddle on the floor. I hoped Mycroft would trip over it after battling his way out of the veil. I hoped he would fall and injure some portion of his stout personage. I hoped the belligerent baron would punch him in the nose. Sherlock must have told my other confounded brother where he might find me. I hated him. Both of them. I had no idea why I sobbed as I ran down the attic stairs.

Shouts rose above and behind me. "After her!"

"Stop that wretched girl!"

"Enola! Wait!" Mycroft's commanding voice.

Muttering something unrepeatable in reply, I plunged down more stairs, and in my stocking feet I slipped and nearly fell, grabbing at the banister to save myself—which gave me the blessed thought to slide down that sturdy, polished wooden rail the rest of the way. I did so, flying through the second storey—I retain a blurred memory of astonished, delighted faces as I whizzed past a group of orphans—and the first storey, to the ground floor. The sounds of footsteps thumping in pursuit faded behind me, and the denizens of the orphanage proper remained upstairs; no one got in my way as I ran through a hallway—some mantles and bonnets hung on pegs; I grabbed one of each—and out the front door.

Slowing to a brisk walk as I crossed the yard, I whisked tears from my cheeks, slung the mantle—a simple navy-blue affair—over my shoulders, and hid my dishevelled hair under an equally simple, old-fashioned dark blue bonnet, probably some matron's Sunday headgear.

Meanwhile, seated in his sheltering box inside the gate, an exceedingly ancient and withered man dozed, his chin propped upon the chest of his brown poplin tunic. Only as I strode quite close to him did he awaken with a start and study me with bleary eyes, his fogged old brain wondering who I was and where I had come from.

As his mouth fumbled open to ask, I told him in my most crisp aristocratic tones, as if I might be a member of the orphanage board or perhaps one of the trustees, "Towheedle, you've been napping again. Shame on you. Open the gate."

Poor man, he jumped to do so.

Next I demanded, "Did a tall gentleman with a limp come this way?"

He nodded, bobbed, pulled at his forelock. "Yes, um . . ." He didn't know whether to call me "ma'am" or "milady."

"And did the girl go with him?"

"The little 'un wit the pink fan? Yes, um . . ."

"Thank you, Towheedle, that will be all."

It really was. All. All right.

All right for Cecily Alistair. Her hair would grow back, and she likewise would grow, coming to terms with herself, finding her place in the world; but first and foremost, she would rejoin her loving mother.

Ah, to have such a mother.

Sailing out of the orphanage, I no longer cared whether the venerable gatekeeper noticed that I wore no shoes. It no longer mattered. Within moments I hailed a cab, which took me to the Underground, which took me to the East End, where I limped to my lodgings, intending to lie down for a well-earned rest. Or, more truthfully, for indulgence in nervous prostration.

As I let myself in at the front door, however, I encountered Mrs. Tupper, who took one look at me and let out a bleat like a sheep. "Miss Meshle! Wot 'appened to you?"

Her question was largely rhetorical, as her deafness, thank goodness, prevented my making any detailed answer. Nevertheless, the dear woman would not take my upraised, dismissive hands for an answer, and hustled me to a seat by the hearth, where she provided me with a basin of warm water in which to soak my insulted feet, a bowl of nourishing if noxious liver-and-barley soup, and a great deal of sympathetic monologue: "The dear alone knows how ye get yerself into these sitchywations, but it's none uv my business, just let me comb out yer poor 'air now, ye'll be needing bag balm an' some cotton lint for them ruined feet, I'll warrant ye went and give your shoes to some poor wretch, ought to 'ave more care for yerself but there ain't a gooder 'eart in London, 'ow ye get yerself all scraped and banged up and yer poor smock torn this way is beyond me, eat yer soup now and there's some bread pudding, poor lamb, yer half starved, wot am I to do wit you?"

But she knew quite well what to do, actually, and by the time I finally thanked her, from the warmth of my bed watched her close my chamber door behind her, and heard her creaking footsteps and plangent voice going down the stairs, I was warmly fed, bathed, and clothed, with my sore feet attended to and my sore heart beginning to feel better as well.

I had felt quite betrayed, you see, because Sherlock had told Mycroft my whereabouts—but my reaction was childish, I realised as I lay trying to compose myself for slumber; Sherlock was only doing his duty as he perceived it, and he had never promised me anything else. In our familial game of hide-and-seek, my brother played fair.

Brothers. Mycroft, too, had done nothing—however annoying—that might not reasonably be expected of him. It was not his fault that he was who he was, any more than it was Mum's fault—

Oh, Mum.

While Mrs. Tupper had mothered me today, where was my real mother? My riddling inquiry,

Narcissus bloomed in water, for he had none.

Chrysanthemum in glass, for she had one.

All of Ivy's tendrils failed to find:
What was the Iris planted behind?

had not yet received any answer. Of course it was too soon to expect one. Perhaps in today's *Pall Mall Gazette.* Closing my eyes, I told myself that I would have a look at it after I napped.

But even when I received my answer, what would the good of it be? Never in her life that I could recall had Mum washed or bandaged or fed me, or combed my hair . . .

My eyes opened, staring at the blank ceiling, and errant tears trickled down my temples.

Very well. I was not going to be able to sleep. Sighing as I wiped the tears away, I got up, found myself a sheaf of foolscap paper and a lap desk, and began to sketch.

I drew an orphan, for I felt like one. Then I drew Lady Cecily all got up as an orphan, for she, a girl lacking a father's love, must feel much as I did. Detailing her sensitive face and brilliant eyes, I thought in how many ways I felt myself a soul-mate to her, and how I had never expected to see her again, yet it had now happened. Therefore might I hope that, perhaps in a few years, when we were grown, we might see each other more often, and perhaps go sketching together?

Meanwhile, Sherlock would make sure she found her way safely to her mother's care. Feeling an odd hiatus in myself as I thought of my brother, I drew a quick caricature of his tall form, and felt my hollow heart fill and warm.

Mycroft's turn. I made quite a brisk study of representing him with a wedding veil draping him to his swollen waistcoat. It made me smile.

Hoping for another reason to smile, next I drew a picture of quite a lovely young lady with gloriously coiffed chestnut hair in which nestled the most dainty and fetching of hats: myself, in a blue promenade gown and quite an expensive wig, with my face disguised by powders and paints and primping plus a parasol. Beautiful, by George, but—but hardly the whole story. I drew myself as a middenpicker, then as Ivy Meshle in her cheap frou-frou and false curls, then as a street stray in a smashed bowler hat, a paragon among ragamuffins—

But this could go on and on. I ought to draw a portrait of Mum.

Taking a fresh sheet of foolscap, I tried, but found I could not. I could not at that moment bring her features to mind.

Instead, within my tentative outline of a feminine head, I filled in other features.

Steady eyes, young yet wise.

Straight nose.

Strong chin.

Quirky mouth. Mona Lisa smile.

An angular face not unlike that of my brother Sherlock, yet quintessentially—my own?

I gawked. Was it really me? Enola?

Never before had I been able to draw myself truly. Why could I do it now?

My own pencilled gaze demanded truth of me.

Because, I admitted—if only to myself—because I knew why the Mona Lisa smiled so oddly. Doubtless she had a mother somewhat like mine. I knew that I would not search for Mum. Not yet, if ever. Not until, or unless, I felt she wanted to see me.

But whether I ever saw her again or not, I was still Enola.

MAY, 1889

IVY MESHLE, AFTER A FEW DAYS BACK AT WORK FOR "Dr. Ragostin," takes pleasure in penning the following letter to "Dr. Ragostin's" client, the general:

Dear Honourable Sir:

Regarding the matter of your missing war memento, to wit, one leg-bone inscribed by the amputating surgeon, Dr. Ragostin is pleased to inform you that he has recovered it from the possession of one Paddy Murphy, cab-driver, who admits to having acquired it by means of your third up-

stairs housemaid, for whom he professed an amorous interest, his scheme being to exhibit it among his low-minded companions for paltry financial gain. If you wish to prosecute the aforementioned Paddy Murphy, a constable may be sent to apprehend him in the Serpentine Mews. Meanwhile, your leg remains in Dr. Ragostin's safekeeping, and you may send for it at your convenience, kindly remitting payment as previously agreed. Dr. Ragostin is delighted to have been able to offer you his trifling assistance, and remain

Sincerely yours,
Leslie T. Ragostin, Ph.D.
as dictated to Miss Ivy Meshle

"My dear Mycroft!" The great detective, Sherlock Holmes, is frankly surprised to find his brother at the door of 221b Baker Street; Mycroft hardly ever deviates from his customary orbit between his government office, his own lodgings, and the Diogenes club. "Come in, have a cigar and a glass of sherry — no? Some urgent wind blows you this way?"

"No, merely a vexing draught beneath the door of my comfort," grumbles Mycroft, settling his bulk in the best armchair.

"May I be of assistance?"

"I doubt it, as you were chump enough to let her go."

"Ah." Sherlock turns away to dig his long fingers into his rather eccentric pipe-tobacco container, a Persian slipper. "Our sister. Am I never to hear the last of the ha-ha incident?"

"Perhaps when I hear the last of the bridal-veil incident. How is Cecily Alistair, by the way?"

"Much better, in the care of her mother and her mother's family. I understand that Lady Theodora is planning a trip to Vienna for herself and her daughter, to consult with the alienists there regarding the young lady's Jekyll-and-Hyde moods."

"Ah. They think her a dual personality?"

"Possibly." Standing on the hearth-rug, Sherlock packs his favourite meerschaum pipe, spilling only a little tobacco in the process.

"Well, certainly an arranged marriage is no cure for that. It was a close thing for her."

"Not really." Puffing to suck the flame into the tobacco, Sherlock lights his pipe with a match, as there is no fire in the hearth at this time of year. "Enola and I had the matter well in hand, and you had no business being there; did I not tell you to stay away?"

"My dear Sherlock, how many times must I tell you? I felt it my duty to *protect* Enola. Do you not shudder at the thought of our sister single-handedly undertaking to trick Viscount Inglethorpe, Baron Merganser, *and* their formidable wives? I could not do otherwise than try to help."

"I doubt that Enola perceives your interference as help." Smoking seems not to soothe Sherlock; indeed, he begins to pace, his long legs taking him across the room and back in a few rapid strides.

Mycroft retorts, "What she perceives is irrelevant, for who is to rescue her from herself if not we, her brothers? I wished to help her that day at the Witherspoon orphanage just as I do now."

"Now?" With droll trepidation Sherlock pauses to eye his older brother. "What ever is she up to now?"

"Why, I wouldn't know. I've had no news of her. It is just this." From his waistcoat pocket Mycroft produces a newspaper clipping and hands it to his brother.

"Ah." Sherlock hands it back, feeling no need to read it, as he has seen it daily in the *Pall Mall Gazette*:

Narcissus bloomed in water, for he had none.

Chrysanthemum in glass, for she had one.

All of Ivy's tendrils failed to find:

What was the Iris planted behind?

Mycroft peers up at him from beneath a thick hedge of eyebrows. "What *was* concealed behind the mirror, Sherlock?"

"Nothing except a considerable sum of money, which I have deposited in a bank for her should she ever need it. Why?"

Mycroft answers the question with another question. "Do you think she placed that advertisement because she needs money?"

"I doubt it. She seems quite able to pay cab-fare generous enough to see her out of many an escapade. In regard to what was behind the mirror, I imagine she is merely curious."

"But why such a strong curiosity?"

"Why not? Curiosity goes hand in hand with intellect, and intellect runs in the family."

"Intellect in a female? Bah. Nonsense, Sherlock; it is some matter of the heart that compels our sister to send our mother another flowery missive. What do you think she wants from this advertisement?"

Frowning, the great detective stands still to look down on his brother, but fails to answer.

Indeed, Mycroft hardly gives him time to answer before he speaks on. "I know what Enola hopes for, and I propose that we should give it to her."

"I fail to follow you."

"Sherlock, it is simple enough. The girl is devoted to her mother, who abandoned her; Enola longs for assurance of her mother's affection. That is what she hopes you found behind the mirror: a love letter from Mummy. And that is what we could provide for her."

Several seconds pass while Sherlock Holmes puffs his meerschaum and stares at his brother. Then he says, not as a question but as a statement, "To bait a trap with, you mean."

"Necessarily so, in order to get her back within the pale of civilised society, provide her with a proper education, see to her future—"

"Desirable as those objectives may be, my dear Mycroft, I think a trick is hardly the way to befriend Enola. I will not lie to her."

"Sherlock! You are saying you will not help me?" A surge of surprised anger lifts Mycroft to his feet at the same time as Sherlock calmly takes a seat.

"That is correct." Sherlock Holmes reaches over to his desk and picks up a slip of foolscap, folding it repeatedly. "Moreover, I have anticipated you. In tomorrow's editions you will see a communication from me. Here is the copy I have kept." He tosses the now-wadded paper across the room to his brother, who succeeds in catching it. Mycroft opens it and reads:

E.H.: Iris was monetary, now planted in Shropshire Royal Bank, your name. Regret can give no further satisfaction. Our mutual friend C.A. thanks you profusely for your gallant assistance, as do I. With utmost regard, S.H.

Mycroft Holmes studies this for some time before he looks up, expressionless.

"Well," he says coldly, "so that's the way it's going to be."

Quite gently, "That's the way it's going to be," says Sherlock.